Boy in Luv

JAY CROWNOVER
and
REBECCA YARROS

D1411544

Cover design by: Mayhem Cover Creations
Editing and Formatting by: Elaine York,
Allusion Graphics, LLC/Publishing & Book Formatting
www.allusiongraphics.com
Proofreading & Copy Editing by: Jenn Wood, All About The Edits

Boy in Luv

Distance sure as hell made his heart grow fonder... But it shattered hers into a million pieces.

Langley Vaughn knows she's never going to make the same mistake again.

Who falls head over heels in love in a week? Langley did, and she's regretted it every day since she handed her heart to a boy with too many secrets and too much baggage. Iker doesn't fit into Langley's world, and he made it clear he doesn't want to. He left before she even got a chance to try and change his mind or to prove to him how good they could be together. Langley's spent the last nine months healing her heart and making big plans for the future. Plans that absolutely don't include Iker... even though he's back, looking better than ever, and saying all the right things.

Iker Alvarez knows he made the biggest mistake of his life.

At first, the pretty blonde in the red dress was nothing more than a means to an end. But, she quickly became so much more. As soon as Iker walked away from Langley, claiming it was for her own good, he knew he screwed up. He left her so she wouldn't worry about him when he deployed, so she wouldn't waste her time waiting around for a guy who was never going to be good enough for her. Only, nine months and a deployment later, Iker still can't get Langley out of his head... and he totally underestimated the hold she has on his hardened heart. He's a guy who's not sure how love should work, or how to go about winning his girl back...he's about to get a crash course in both.

Chapter 1

"**I**'m glad you didn't die."

The words were spoken softly and without a hint of humor. They were followed by a loud sniff and my little brother trying to subtly wipe at his eyes so I wouldn't notice the fact he was fighting back tears. He was serious. He said the same words to me every single time I came back from a deployment, no matter what condition I returned in. And he always cried, which meant I always had to fight back tears of my own.

I hooked an arm around Gael's neck and rubbed the knuckles of my free hand against the top of his head, clearing my throat so I could speak through the emotion caught there.

"Me too, kid. I told you I would be back in one piece. You know I always keep my word." I wasn't a guy who made promises I couldn't keep, and I refused to let my baby brother down. Everything I did, every choice I made—both good and bad—were so that Gael could have a better life. So he could do more, be more, and live beyond the means I'd always felt held me back when I was his age.

Promising him over and over again nothing would happen to me while I was deployed to some of the most dangerous places in the world was the only time I made a vow, knowing I might not be able to come through in the end. But the words made us feel better, even if we both recognized how empty and useless they were at the end of the day.

I was lucky homecoming coincided with Gael's first summer break from college. I'd spent nine months living in an emotional kaleidoscope of fear, anger, boredom, and regret. Seeing my baby brother struggling to look tough and keep his tears in check instantly launched me back into protective big brother mode and sent me crashing back to reality. I was no longer just a soldier, a cog in the machine of war. Now, seeing Gael instantly forced all the feelings I'd purposely locked down and hid away when I had a job to do, back to the surface. Far earlier than I was ready for.

I left my truck with him when I left for the desert and he'd surprised me by driving halfway across the country and meeting me as soon as my boots were back on Colorado soil. This wasn't my first or last deployment. But, it was the first time I'd ever come back and had someone I loved waiting for me. I purposely kept my ties to others minimal and loose. I didn't want anyone waiting around, living half a life, while I was in some God-forsaken place, dodging bullets and doing things I couldn't talk about. I usually even encouraged my brother and my grandmother—the only family I had—to give me a few weeks to decompress and shift out of survival mode before coming to visit me, or before I would make the trip home after a deployment.

Gael showing up unannounced was one more reminder my little brother wasn't exactly so little anymore. In fact, he seemed to have grown a couple of inches while I was away. He almost met me eye to eye now, and since we were on the same level, there was no missing the exhaustion and worry coloring his watery gaze.

I used my hold on his neck to drag him toward my... his...truck. I knew he was going to try and leave the truck with me whenever he decided to leave, but I wasn't going to take it. He needed it more than I did, and it was important to me Gael never wanted for anything.

"Thanks for coming, but let's get out of here. I'm starving." I also wanted to sleep for a solid week so I could reset. "I can't believe you came for the homecoming ceremony."

The shock of seeing my baby brother in the crowd of excited wives and girlfriends and crying kids had finally worn off. If Gael and I didn't look so much alike, I might've missed him altogether because I was conditioned to ignore the pang of remorse that I never let anyone in, never let anyone get close enough to wait for me. If one of my fellow soldiers hadn't elbowed me and muttered, "Alvarez, is that your brother? He looks just like you," I would've totally overlooked Gael.

"I've wanted to come for a long time." Gael pushed out of my headlock and lifted a hand to brush his hair back from his forehead. "You're always so secretive and private when it comes to what you're doing and where you're going. I grew up with you knowing every single move I made. It never seemed very fair that I've always been on the outside looking in when it comes to you."

He'd always been a scarily smart kid, but he was now growing into an incredibly good-looking and well-rounded young man. Seeing him so composed and no longer looking at me like I hung the moon and had all the answers to everything in the universe sent warm tendrils of pride skittering through me. Maybe, just possibly, I'd done an all-right job raising the kid. Maybe it was time to breathe a little easier and start working at building a life of my own.

"I don't think I've ever had a choice to make that wasn't hard. I doubt I've gotten it right every single time, but you know, everything I've ever done, I always put you and your future first." I dragged a hand down my face, knowing I looked gaunt and tired. "I'm not exactly at my best when I get back from a deployment." It would take weeks until I started to feel like myself again.

My brother snorted and bumped me with his shoulder. I stumbled a little at the contact and heard Gael suck in a breath in surprise. Out of the corner of my eye, I watched as he shook his head. "Iker." His tone was low and serious. "I don't always need your best. After everything, after all you've done for me, all you've sacrificed..." I got another head shake and a narrow-eyed look. "I think you can cut yourself some slack."

He shook the keys in his hand in front of my face and shot me a lopsided grin. "You look like you're about to fall over. Let's get some food and I'll take you home."

I sighed and nodded. I'd subleased my apartment while I was gone, so I really had no idea what "home" was going to look like, or what condition it was going to be in. But the thought of sleeping in my own bed was enough to make me ignore any lingering worries. There were all kinds of little details I needed to take care of, now that I was back on my home turf. Like getting my cell phone turned back on. I was going to have to move that to the top of my to-do list.

Seeing Gael's iPhone sticking out of his back pocket, I made a "gimme" gesture and ordered him to hand the device over. Being a typical teenager, he resisted at first, asking a million questions about what I wanted his phone for. I'd rather have all my teeth pulled out with a rusty pair of pliers before I told him the truth. It was tricky to admit to myself I wanted his phone to check up on a girl I had no right to still be thinking about. And no, there was no way I could wait until tomorrow to creep on her social media. The itch had been under my skin since the minute I walked away from her. If I was going to be honest about what I was up to, Gael would know exactly what I was like when I wasn't at my best, and I wasn't sure I was ready for him to see those jagged, uneven parts of me.

After a short wrestling match, which I was going to win, no matter what, I got my hands on the phone. I pushed Gael toward the truck as I tapped on the screen, pulling up her info as my heart felt like it was tying itself into a million knots.

I sighed when I saw her face. It'd been nine months, but it was burned on my brain. I could still see her sleepy, soft face, so innocent and unassuming. She had no idea I was going to leave her behind, that I always planned to walk away from her. She never asked, but I lied by omission, nonetheless.

Langley Vaughn. Her name was as fancy, high-class, and unique as she was. She started way the hell out of my league, and I'd made sure it ended with her knowing exactly why the two of us could never work out. However, despite the purposeful and possibly cruel steps I'd taken to make sure she didn't waste any more time hung up on me, I couldn't stop thinking about her. I was really good at pushing everything and anyone who was a distraction out of my mind while I did what I had to do. But Langley Vaughn was the exception. She was always there, hovering, lurking, clinging to my every thought and feeling. I'd forced her to let me go, but I'd been unable to the same.

Her sunshiny blonde hair was shorter than when I left her alone in that king-sized bed. She looked a little thinner, and I could tell her smile was forced in a handful of the photos she had posted on Instagram. I absently rubbed at the spot on my chest where my heart clenched painfully when I noticed in most of her current photos, she looked genuinely happy and carefree. I told myself over and over again it would be better if she got over me, but I guess I wasn't really prepared to witness the proof she had.

Sighing, I handed the phone back to my brother, noticing we hadn't moved because he was too busy watching what I was doing over my shoulder. He tapped his phone on his thigh and asked, "Does she have anything to do with you managing to pay off my tuition last-minute, when that grant I was counting on fell through my first semester?" His dark eyebrows lifted, and I silently cursed him for always being so damn smart and perceptive. "You told me before you left you had a funny story to tell me. It doesn't look like you're very amused, though."

I sighed again and closed my eyes. I tilted my head to the side so it could rest against the passenger's side window. "I needed money fast, and she has a lot of it. She needed a date who would rub her very rich family the wrong way, and I was free. Our paths should've never crossed, but they did." And I'd felt off-balance and uneasy ever since. "She's a good girl. Sweet as can be."

Gael started the truck and muttered something I couldn't hear under his breath. I cracked open an eye and gave him a questioning look. "What did you say?"

He frowned as he maneuvered my truck from the parking spot, out into the flow of traffic. "You like her."

It wasn't a question. Which was a good thing, because the last thing I wanted to do was start lying to the one person who could see through me.

"Yeah. I like her." More than liked her. She was the one person I wanted to hold onto, even though I knew she had been slipping through my fingers from the start. "Doesn't matter. I made sure she doesn't like me anymore before I left. I didn't tell her I was deploying and dipped out on her almost as soon as she decided she could lean on me and trust me."

"Are you going to let her know you're back? Maybe explain why you left the way you did." It was hard to hear the hope in his voice. It was even more difficult to keep that same feeling from taking root in my heart.

Squeezing my eyes and letting my hands curl into loose fists, I muttered, "She's better off without me." Because, unlike him, Langley had seen me at my worst. She knew I could play the role of the villain, just as easily as I jumped in to be the hero.

It looked like she'd already started to move on with her life, and it would be best if I did the same thing.

I reached out a hand and clapped it on the back of my baby brother's neck. "Feed me, kid. I'm dying over here."

It was a clumsy way to change the subject, but effective. Gael fell silent and I realized our roles had flipped.

I was used to being the one taking care of and constantly worrying about him. Today, Gael was the one who showed up and proceeded to take care of me. It was the first time I came back from an active war zone and had someone there to keep me upright and steady while the world shifted and settled around me.

The only person who would ever know I secretly wondered what it would feel like if it was an elegant, classy blonde waiting for me instead of my baby brother, was me.

Chapter 2

Langley

"You're certain you won't let me throw you a party?" Dad asked as I locked my apartment door.

"Nope." I nearly dropped the phone from where I had it wedged between my ear and shoulder as I struggled with the deadbolt. It slid home and I grabbed my messenger bag from the hallway floor as my neighbor passed without waving.

I waved at them anyway.

Maybe it wasn't the friendliest building in downtown Colorado Springs, but it sure beat the sorority house. Not that I hadn't enjoyed living with forty-four of my Greek sisters the last couple of years. Having every meal prepared was a definite bonus, especially during finals; however, I wasn't exactly setting myself up for adulthood if I couldn't manage to make my own grilled cheese. After living solo this last year, I wasn't a half-bad cook. *MasterChef* wasn't banging down my door or anything, but I survived.

"Nope, meaning you won't let me throw you one, or no, you're not certain you want one?"

"No, you can't throw me a party." I grinned and shook my head, even though he couldn't see me.

Pretty sure everyone on this side of the Rockies heard my father's overly dramatic sigh of disappointment.

"Come on, you hate parties just as much as I do." I opened the door to the stairwell and clicked my way down a flight of stairs in my favorite pair of red-soled heels.

"Not when I get to celebrate my daughter graduating college, I don't. Maybe I want to shout it from the rooftops. You know how proud I am of you, Langley."

"I do, and I appreciate it." I pushed through the door that led straight into the parking lot and headed for my car. "Just having you at graduation is enough to make me happy."

"Make sure she gets those seats!" I heard Virginia call through the phone.

Not having to live with my stepmother during breaks and holidays away from school was yet another perk of having my own apartment.

"I'll do no such thing," Dad answered. It came through muffled, like he held his hand over the phone's mic. "I don't give a damn if Camille thinks it's too far to walk. No, Virginia, she does not qualify for special consideration."

I unlocked my car and swung my bag into the passenger seat before climbing behind the wheel as they continued bickering.

"Because she's pregnant, not disabled!" he barked. "And if she were the one graduating, maybe I'd care. Tell her to wear some flats and deal with it."

"Dad, I need to head out to my interview," I said, when there was a lull in their back and forth. The engine purred to life, and I made my way out of the lot as the call connected through my Bluetooth.

"Right, I'm sorry. At least let me take you to dinner. You and your boyfriend. What was his name? Steve? Simon?" His voice came through the speakers, full of amusement.

"Yes, Sam's coming tomorrow, but he isn't my boyfriend, remember?" I pulled out into traffic and checked the clock. Good, I left myself a good twenty-minute buffer before my interview. And sure, maybe it was only ten minutes away...in really heavy traffic, but you never got a second chance to make the best impression, and I sure as hell wasn't going to be late. I wanted this internship more than anything. I would have even put up with living with Virginia for the summer if it meant I got to put Overland Financial on my resume.

Don't go that far.

"Right. Sam isn't your boyfriend, he's just a guy you see from time to time. What do you call that?" Dad's sarcasm wasn't lost on me.

"Casual, Dad. I call it casual. I also call it a huge regret that I even mentioned him to you." Dad had gone all background-check crazy the moment I'd mentioned I had a date last month. Sam and I weren't exclusive, or labeled. We just happened to date every once in a while. He was the perfect distraction when I needed it the most.

"Is she still seeing that construction worker?" Virginia bellowed.

"Electrician," I answered, not that it mattered. Anyone who worked with their hands didn't count as a worthwhile human in Virginia's book, unless they were using their hands to count money.

"Oh, come on, Langley!" Virginia's voice was shrill in the background. "Let me set you up with one of the guys from the club. You know, June Maxfield's boy is graduating from Harvard this weekend, and he'll be home for the summer."

"Henry Maxfield is an asshole. No, thank you," I replied, then winced. Over the last nine months, I'd gotten better at speaking my mind...a little too good sometimes. Luckily, Dad just laughed, and I heard the distinct sound of a door shutting. "I like Sam just fine."

Sam was nice. Kind. Smart. Called when he said he would. Showed up when he said he would. Never pressured me to give more than I was willing. There was a whole list of qualities I liked about Sam. Plus, he was here. He wasn't off fighting in a war halfway across the world he hadn't even bothered to tell me about while I'd been busy falling in love with him.

Not like some other guys I'd dated. Fake dated. Whatever the hell it had been. I was no longer hung up on Iker Alvarez. No longer losing sleep over him. No longer thinking about him every minute of every day...just every other minute.

"I'm sure you like Sam. He must be a good guy if you've been out with him a few times now." His tone sagged, and I pictured him flopping into his leather office chair. "I was just wondering if maybe you'd heard from—"

"Do not finish that sentence," I warned as I pulled up to a red light. "No, I haven't heard. No, he hasn't reached out. Just let it go, Dad. I sure as hell have." Or so I tried to convince myself, time and time again. Some days, the lie was easier to buy than others.

"Yeah, it definitely sounds like you have." His sarcasm dripped about as thick as molasses.

My hands clenched on the steering wheel as I shoved every single thought and memory of *him* as far from my consciousness as possible. Not going there. Not when I was finally healed and happy.

"Sorry, honey," Dad said softly, after another few seconds of silence.

Someone honked behind me and I startled. Right, the light was green. Green meant go. Green did not mean lament about guys who never gave a shit about you.

"It's okay," I told Dad as I turned into the parking lot in front of the office building I'd been staring at all year. "I just pulled in, so I'm going to head up for my interview."

"I still don't understand why you won't take an internship at Vaughn Holdings? I happen to know the owner would love to take you on."

Like a magnet, my attention hopped across the street to the taller building that housed Dad's firm. It would have been so much easier to say yes to him. To slide into the position that had been earmarked for me since birth. Dad probably had a nameplate engraved with my name on it already and everything.

It would have made him so happy if I accepted his offer.

But somewhere in the last year, I'd stopped prioritizing everyone else's happiness above my own. Not that selfishness was my goal, but not being a martyr any longer was now definitely up there, right behind breathing and eating.

"Dad, you know I want to do this on my own," I said gently.

JAY CROWNOVER *and* REBECCA YARROS

"But you don't have to, Langley. I'm incredibly proud that you're independent and driven. Really, I am. But you're a Vaughn. Generations of Vaughns have sacrificed to get us where we are, to make sure you don't have to start the ballgame taking a fastball."

"I'd hardly call my trust fund and upbringing taking a fastball. More like starting on third with a lead and the coach screaming at me to head for home." Not like *him*— the one I refused to think about. *He* hadn't even started the ballgame on the field. No, he'd clawed his way into the park and been forced to prove himself before anyone had even deemed him worthy of a bat.

I hated that I'd admired him for it.

Hated that he'd hijacked my train of thought yet again.

"Fair point. I just hate knowing that I can make your life easier and you won't let me. That's pretty much a dad's entire job, you know."

I glanced at the clock. Still fifteen minutes early.

"A dad's entire job is to raise a decent human being." Which he had. Sure, I got jealous from time to time, and even petty, but I'd like to think I was on the okay side of the moral compass. "You know I love you for wanting to help me, but this is something I really need to do on my own."

He sighed. "Okay. I respect that. Tell Peter I said hello."

My stomach clenched. "Tell me you did not call Peter Overland and tell him that I'm interviewing!"

"Of course not." Dad scoffed. "But if you think he won't put two and two together, then you're sorely

14

underestimating him. Now go take on the world, Tiger. I'll see you at graduation tomorrow."

"I'll be the one in black." I spoke fluent sarcasm as well.

"Love you." He chuckled.

Echoing the sentiment, I hung up and killed the engine. After I took a moment to straighten my blouse and skirt, I headed into the building with a lot more confidence than I was actually feeling.

The lobby was quiet for a Friday afternoon, and my heels echoed on the marble as I walked toward the elevator.

Wait. Was twelve minutes early too early? Would it say I was organized and ready? Or desperate and bored? Five minutes would be better.

I sat in one of the arm chairs that faced a wishing fountain and debated throwing my entire trust fund in with the hopes I'd land this internship.

That would have been a major disappointment to the two college students that trust fund was currently putting through school, so it probably wasn't the best idea. Then again, as of tomorrow I was a graduate, and paying off the entirety of the balance on Gael's tuition last week had been a no-brainer. I had money. He didn't. It wasn't like I couldn't take the financial hit. Hell, I made that much in interest over a year's time.

At least his brother won't have to gigolo himself out for his brother's education ever again.

I hadn't done it for *him*, though. I'd made the call and dropped the cash because the kid was smart, ambitious, and deserved to start the ballgame at least on first base.

15

Both of the kids I decided to help out did. *All* kids wanting to pursue higher education did.

Hoping to soothe my nerves, I took out my phone and opened my Instagram, scrolling through my latest notifications. When I noticed one of my sorority sisters had liked an older picture on my feed, I clicked on the image out of force of habit to see what had caught her eye. Or rather, who...

Iker Alvarez.

So much for not thinking about him when I couldn't bring myself to erase him totally from my life.

My chest tightened as those deep brown eyes stared out at me from the picture he'd snapped the night I'd met him. Why didn't I just delete the post and spare myself this scab-breaking open sensation of loss? For the same reason I kept that stupid, wonderful letter he'd left the morning hesnuck out on me. It wasn't in a place of honor or anything. I shoved it into my glove box, between my owner's manual and the map Dad insisted I carry even with the GPS, and had simply forgotten to throw it out.

Liar.

I cursed the sorority sister who'd liked the picture, but didn't look away. I'd never been able to look away from Iker, which had been half of my freaking problem. The guy was gorgeous. The other half of my issue stemmed from the fact he was just as beautiful on the inside as he was out. With the exception that he'd left me naked and sleeping in a five-star resort while he snuck out, breaking my heart in the process. Yeah, that took the "pretty on the inside" factor down a notch.

My thumb hovered over the option to delete the picture, but I couldn't. Besides Camille's wedding pictures—which I didn't spend time fawning over—it was one of the only pieces of tangible evidence Iker even existed.

Noting the time, I stood and sent up a quick prayer he still existed somewhere, that he hadn't been yet another casualty in a war the news didn't even bother covering anymore. Not that anyone would even think to tell me if something had happened to him. I was nothing to him, and I had to remind myself he was no longer allowed to be everything to me.

The elevator ride was short, and I arrived at the reception desk for Overland Financial exactly six minutes early for my interview. I used those six minutes to mentally prepare, which was ten thousand times harder with Iker's memory shoving every thought to the side and causing general chaos in my brain.

By minute seven, I sat across from Peter Overland, my father's local rival.

By minute ten, we'd gone over my resume and fascination with hedge fund management.

"So, tell me, Ms. Vaughn, why manage money?" he asked, peering over thin-framed glasses at me. His stare cut me to the quick, and I got the feeling he saw way more than applicants wanted him to. He had his pick of any polished, educated, smooth graduate whom he wanted. I could give him the canned, easy answer, and still have a shot at the internship.

But if I'd wanted easy, I would be over at Vaughn Enterprises.

"I like money," I told him truthfully. "It has tremendous potential for good when grown and nurtured carefully."

"Potential for good?" He leaned back in his chair, taking my resume with him.

"Yes, sir. I've learned over the last year that my income, when carefully tended, gives me the opportunity to invest in charity. To do more with it than spend it frivolously."

His silver brows puckered. "When tended. Why not simply give it all to charity? Wouldn't you argue that has a greater benefit?"

"Sure. Once. But by growing income, we can invest in good works consistently, without threatening future donations. In fact, I would argue that with precise and careful management, we can invest even more." My body clamored to shift positions, but I refused to give away my nerves by fidgeting.

"Interesting."

I had zero clue if he was being sarcastic or not.

"So, Ms. Vaughn. Are you any relation to Corbin Vaughn?"

"We share a few genes." I kept my eyes on him, ignoring the instinct to glance through his corner office windows at Dad's firm across the street.

His eyebrows rose, but that was the only outward sign he'd even heard me. "Your GPA is impressive, but so is every other candidate who walks into this room. So, I'll ask you the same question I asked them."

"Perfect." Good thing my skirt was black, because I knew my sweaty palms would have left giant handprints on the material.

"What's the most daring investment you've made personally?" He leaned forward and placed my resume on the shiny expanse of mahogany desk separating us.

Iker's face came to mind. Well, at least this would distinguish me from the rest. Either he'd laugh, or he'd send me packing. "I paid a stranger to be my date to my sister's wedding."

Mr. Overland's eyes widened and sparked with what I hoped was interest.

"It was a ten-thousand-dollar investment made for the singular purpose of shaking up my family and paying my stepsister back for being terrible to me. While the dividends weren't seen financially, they were certainly felt in exactly the manner I'd anticipated while striking the deal." It was a ten-thousand-dollar investment I'd never once regretted making. Even on the darkest, hardest days, when I was certain I'd never stop hurting, I still hadn't regretted it.

"And did you feel personally satisfied with the outcome of your investment?" A corner of his mouth lifted.

"I can admit that it left me just as shaken as the rest of my family. But it also opened my eyes and brought me into an awareness of the world that I'm not sure I would have been able to attain with it. Without him." Sure, the deal had been an investment, but I couldn't keep calling Iker *it*.

"Hmmmm." Mr. Overland hummed softly, looking over my resume. Then he looked up at me and nodded once, making a decision I could only guess at. "Ms. Vaughn, I'm not going to offer you the hedge fund internship."

My heart plummeted eight stories and splattered on the pavement below. Raising my chin, I gave him a smile my mother would have been proud of. "I understand."

"Instead, I'm going to offer you a full-time position in our Central Texas office. We have an entire fund there dedicated to charitable giving that could use another team member. I think you might find that much more to your liking, and I'd personally like to see if you can use that precise and careful input you mentioned to help grow that fund, so we can do more of that consistent giving." He smiled, the skin at the corner of his eyes crinkling.

I sputtered and accepted the offer with thanks and zero hesitation. There was a lot of thanks, the reality of having to move to a new state where I didn't know anyone not fully sinking in. It was all a happy blur from that moment on. This was an absolute dream come true! I'd be working in the field I loved, not just to make money for people who already had enough, but to better the lives of those who didn't.

I broke into foot-stomping giddy laughter when I reached my car, my offer letter firmly tucked away in my messenger bag. Holy crap, I was graduating college tomorrow and moving to Texas within the next month.

Good thing I'd kept things casual with Sam. I knew how hard it was to be left behind by someone you were in love with. The last thing I needed was an emotional complication like that with my entire future on the line.

Chapter 3

Iker

"You slept for almost two days straight, and you still look like crap." I blinked up at Gael as he plopped a mug of coffee on the table in front of me.

I rubbed my hands over my face and stifled a yawn. Everything in my body still felt heavy and lethargic. I had no idea what time it was, or even what day it was. My mind felt like it was wrapped up in clinging, inescapable webs woven out of remorse and regret. I shook my head back and forth, trying to dislodge some of the fog of doubt I was straining to see through.

"I told you it took me a minute to get my footing after I get back." I picked up the mug and sighed contentedly as the warmth seeped into my palms. "I bet you're bored out of your mind. You came all this way to see me, and I've been no fun."

Gael snorted and leaned forward so he could brace his hands on the cheap countertop separating us. "I came to make sure you were okay, and to say thank you for fixing everything for me before school started last semester. I wanted you to see with your own eyes that I'm doing okay. I wanted to prove to you that you no longer have to put your neck on the line for every little thing." His eyes shifted downward and I squinted as he shifted his weight nervously. "There's something I have to tell you."

I rubbed my eyes again and put down the coffee. Gael was always serious, but the expression on his face right now had a chill shooting up my spine. I knew I wasn't going to like whatever it was he had to say next.

"You won't ever have to do anything sketchy to pay for my tuition again." Gael lifted his head and blew out a breath. "All four years of my undergrad have been paid for. No more scrambling with financial aid and counting on grants and scholarships that might not come through. No worrying about the crushing weight of student debt when I'm done with school."

I felt my eyes pop wide and my heart started to pound erratically in my chest. "What? How? Who?" My tongue tripped over the words and the chill spread throughout my body because I was pretty sure I knew the answer to the last question.

"I went to the financial aid office to make sure I applied for every grant and special funding I could as soon as the semester started. I didn't want to end up in the same boat as before. I didn't want you worrying while you were deployed. The financial aid officer informed me that I was selected by a private donor to receive a full-ride scholarship. Only me and one other kid in the country were chosen for this special scholarship opportunity. The school wouldn't give out any information on the donor, obviously, but I'm smart enough to put two and two together after hearing you talk about Langley."

Was it possible? Had Langley paid for my brother's entire education, even after everything I'd done to her? No one could be that kind, that selfless...could they?

Struck speechless, I stared at my brother in silence while my mind raced to catch up with and process this new information.

Gael raised a hand and rubbed the back of his neck anxiously. "I know you probably won't like it, but I want to see her, and tell her thank you before I leave Colorado. I want to thank her for the opportunities I'm going to have, and for opening doors I doubt I'd be able to open on my own." He sighed heavily. "I also want to thank her for taking such a huge responsibility off your plate. You have a chance to finally focus on yourself. You never would've stopped putting me first if she didn't come into the picture. We owe her more than we can ever repay."

I felt like I couldn't breathe. I put my palm on my chest and pushed against the spot where my heart was racing.

"I... She's not going to want to see me, Gael." My voice cracked but I was still reeling from the bomb Gael dropped, so I couldn't be embarrassed by it.

"Yeah, maybe not. You pulled a super dick move on her, but don't you want to apologize?" He walked around the counter and pulled out the barstool next to mine. "The number-one lesson I learned from watching you, is that doing the right thing isn't always easy. Most of the time, doing the right thing hurts worse than the consequences from doing the wrong thing.

"It would've been so easy for you to fall into a different lifestyle, growing up where we did. But, you always did the right thing, even if it meant you suffered. This girl deserves an apology, and she has the right to every ounce of gratitude we both have. It's not often guys like us, guys who come from nothing, run into an actual guardian angel."

I swore under my breath and dropped my forehead so it banged painfully on the countertop. "It's not like I can just call her up and ask her to meet me for coffee. I ghosted her in the worst way possible. She doesn't even know that I'm back, or that I'm still breathing." She looked perfectly happy and her life had obviously moved on. Who was I, other than a bad memory she probably wanted to forget forever.

Gael tapped his fingers on the table and looked at me with an arched eyebrow. "Coming up with complex battle strategies is part of your job. Are you really going to sit there and tell me you can't figure out a way to fix this? Are you scared?"

I *was* scared. Terrified. There wasn't much in my life I hadn't been able to withstand, but seeing disappointment and disgust in Langley's pretty blue eyes was something I was sure I wouldn't be able to come back from. However, there was no way I was letting my baby brother know any of that.

Swearing again, I banged my forehead on the counter a second time and muttered, "She's graduating. I saw a post on her Instagram when I was creeping on your phone the other day. Might be better to try and see her somewhere where there's other people around." After all, she wasn't shy when it came to making a scene. The girl was big on leaving a lasting impression. "She'll probably be excited since she's done with school."

Showing up unannounced while she was celebrating something so monumental might be a solid plan of attack. Then again, it might ruin her entire day. But, like Gael said, doing the right thing was rarely the easy choice to make.

Gael banged a hand on the table, making me flinch. "Let's go. You know which school she goes to, right? We can find whatever we need to find her on the internet."

I groaned, resigned to the fact we were really doing this now that I'd thrown the idea out there. My brother wasn't going to let it go, and honestly, neither was my conscience. I did owe Langley more than I would ever be able to repay. She deserved so much more than an apology, but it was a place to start when it came to clearing the debt.

"It's not a funeral. Don't look so grumpy. Go take a shower and I'll make something to eat." He nudged me out of the chair, eyes already on his phone as he cyber-stalked Langley. Once again, I was overwhelmed with how good it felt to have someone looking after me when I was at my most unguarded and vulnerable. He was finally old enough, it really felt like I had someone unshakeable on my side.

In the shower, it was impossible to stop the flood of memories from overtaking my every thought.

I could clearly recall Langley's bright smile when she let the mask of perfection she wore slip, and let it shine. I could still feel how silky and soft her hair was wrapped around my hands and trailing across my skin. I was never going to forget how she tasted and felt in my arms. The sweet, sexy sounds she made when she lost herself to passion and desire were going to echo in my ears forever. I'd had more than one dream that'd forced me to wake up hard and aching because all I had as a reminder of her were those lingering memories. I'd never be on the receiving end of the real thing again.

Unfortunately, while my brain understood I'd screwed up and ruined any chance I had with everyone's real-life dream girl, my dick hadn't got the memo. Any time Langley crossed my mind, my body almost immediately responded. Sure, the opportunity to get over her by getting someone else under me had been limited due to my deployment, but the truth was, I hadn't even been tempted. I'd always been a guy who was somewhat of a player. I knew I wasn't going to settle down and commit, so I typically had no problem living the hit-it-and-quit-it lifestyle.

Until Langley.

She was impossible for me to quit and my dick wasn't all that interested in a cheap knockoff. My hand and my memories were going to have to do when it came to getting off. I was hopeful that seeing her face-to-face would bring the closure I needed to get back to my old self. If I could see her hatred up close and personal, it would be the motivation I needed to move on.

I was still grouchy when I got out of the shower, but seeing an outfit laid out on the bed when I walked into my bedroom was enough to pull a weak grin from me. Gael picked out one of the few button-down shirts Langley insisted on buying for me when we were trying to fool her family into thinking we were together, and a pair of black jeans. He was obviously worried about making a good impression on the woman responsible for securing his future.

Figuring it wouldn't hurt anything for me to follow his lead, I shaved and styled my hair...what little of it I had after being in the desert for so long. I rolled up the sleeves of the shirt, exposing the heavily tattooed length of my forearms. I thought about rolling them back down so I didn't draw any attention to myself, but quickly discarded the idea. I was who I was. Generally, I liked the guy I was on a day-to-day basis, but I knew he could use some improvement. Apologizing for the way I treated Langley was a step in the right direction of being a better man. It wouldn't lift the weight of guilt off of me, but it would alleviate it some, which was all I needed. I was being crushed by it, suffocated.

Another halfhearted grin slipped out when I walked into the living room of the apartment. Gael was dressed fairly similar to me, only he had a jaunty bowtie added to his ensemble. He would fit right in at a private college graduation.

My brother was chatty on the way to the college. He was obviously excited and nervous. Langley really was a savior in his eyes. For having never met her, Gael spoke of her glowingly. It was hard to hear. I was used to being his ultimate hero, the one who made sure he never wanted for anything. It was a tough pill to swallow to hear him be in awe of someone else, mostly because that someone else had turned my life and heart upside-down with minimal effort. I'd given up the right to sing Langley's praises, so it rubbed me the wrong way my brother could do it so freely.

It took a minute to find a place to park. We got a couple looks from people as we maneuvered through the sprawling, downtown campus. The graduation ceremony was usually held on one of the quads on campus, so I followed the sounds of cheering until we found the right one. We arrived just as the commencement closing was happening. A sharp pang of sadness shot through me when I realized I was too late to see Langley walk across the stage and get her diploma. It seemed I was always just a little too late and never quite good enough when it came to her.

After the explosive cheers from the graduates and the spectacle of the caps being thrown in the air, the crowd started to move and shift as families started to gather to congratulate their loved ones. By sheer coincidence, I happened to catch sight of Langley's father and stepmother. Her dad caught my eye, and I watched the smile on his face drop off as recognition hit him.

I liked Langley's dad. He was a good man and also a fellow military man. He didn't blink an eye when Langley brought me home to cause trouble. In fact, all he wanted was for his daughter to be happy. For her to be looked over and cared for. I did all of that, until I hadn't. If I were in his shoes, I'd want to kick my ass too.

The older man took a step in my direction, but was almost immediately jerked back by his snotty, bitchy wife. There was no love lost between us when it came to Langley's stepmother. The woman was a piece of work, treating Langley like an intruder in her own home. Corbin Vaughn craned his neck to keep me in his sights as he was forcibly dragged away.

I heaved a deep sigh and went to point out Langley's family to Gael, only to realize my brother was no longer at my side. I turned in a semi-circle to see where he went, and froze when a familiar, sunny blonde head suddenly appeared in the crowd.

"Iker?"

I froze at the sound of my name, body going ice-cold and boiling hot at the same time. I couldn't move. Couldn't look away from her. I was torn between wanting to run toward her to close the distance between us, and ducking down so I could hide in the throng of people surrounding us.

It took a full minute for my brain to compute that while it was my name Langley was calling, she hadn't seen me and wasn't looking in my direction at all. A moment later, Gael was standing in front of her, sticking out a hand for her to shake. Those baby blue eyes of hers were twice their normal size, and I could see confusion coloring them, even with the space between us.

I was too far away to hear what they were saying to each other. Gael was more animated than he ever was, hands moving wildly as he spoke. Langley looked adorably baffled, then happy, then heartbroken. She also looked really good in her graduation cap and gown. Gael hooked a thumb over his shoulder in my direction, and I went still as stone as my gaze locked with Langley's.

I watched her put a hand to her chest and all the color bleed from her flawless, unforgettable face. She wobbled a little on those sky-high heels she liked to wear, and one of her hands shot out to lock on my little brother's forearm. I wanted to scream at her to let him go. I wanted to tell her

29

she could hold onto me instead. I knew the words were useless, though. My actions spoke so much louder.

I was yelling at myself to move, to do something, do anything, when a guy who appeared to be around my age suddenly appeared behind Langley. He gave my brother a curious look, and my blood turned into lava as he threw an arm around Langley's shoulder in a way which was annoyingly familiar and comfortable. The guy was big. He had a head full of blond hair, and a beard. He also had a tattoo on the side of his neck and on the back of the hand that was dangling over Langley's shoulders. He didn't look anything like her douchebag ex who was now married to her stepsister. This guy would fit in at any dive bar or pool hall in the city. I had no clue who he was or why he was so touchy-feely with Langley, but I hated him on sight. I wanted to break the arm he had wrapped around her and crush the fingers which were so free to touch her.

"Iker? What are you doing here?"

Lost in thought and caught up in my own jealousy, I didn't realize the three of them had moved closer to where I was standing. Gael moved to my side, giving me a nudge as a reminder to get my shit together.

I had to clear my throat a couple of times before I could force the words out. The sight of Langley with another guy totally blew all my reasons for being here out of the water. I was having a hard time focusing on anything other than all the places where she was pressed against a man who wasn't me.

"Uh...congratulations on your graduation. Gael came to town when I got back and really wanted a chance to meet you. Sorry for popping up unannounced." It sounded so lame and pathetic. Why couldn't I just tell her how much

I missed her, how sorry I was for screwing up as badly as I had?

Awkward silence fell over our group until I blurted out, "I'm so sorry, Langley," at the exact same time she muttered, "I'm so glad you're alive, Iker."

We stared at each other for a long time, both of us breathing hard as the crowd and chaos faded away. I was trying to figure out what else to say when the guy whom we'd both been ignoring pulled Langley closer and dropped a possessive kiss on the top of her head.

I automatically stiffened and heard Gael grumble something under his breath. Beard-o grunted and spoke loud enough there was no way I could pretend I didn't hear him.

"Let's go, Langley. Your family is waiting for us. We don't want to keep your dad waiting, do we?"

The message was clear. He was the one in her life now. She was his. I couldn't hold back a full-body cringe when he shifted to take her hand.

Langley blinked like she'd been in a daze and slowly nodded.

"Seriously, thank you for everything." Gael reached out a hand, which she shook automatically. Her manners and politeness were an inherent part of who she was, after all.

Our eyes met briefly once again and a small, lopsided smile pulled at her mouth. "It was nice to see you...both. Take care."

She turned and walked away with blond, tattooed guy, her hand remaining in his.

Gael had to hold me upright as my knees turned into jelly after I could no longer see her.

Watching her walk away without chasing after her and begging for forgiveness was one of the hardest things I'd ever done. It felt like I had a wide-open hole in the center of my chest. Now that I realized how important she was, and how much of my heart she had a hold on, this goodbye burned its way through my blood. My ignorance and arrogance made the last one more bearable. But this girl got to me in no time at all.

The pain was what I deserved. I could admit it. I hated I now knew firsthand just how badly I'd made her feel when I left.

I rubbed my forehead and muttered, "I need a drink. Many drinks."

Gael chuckled and tossed his arm over my shoulders. "The right thing is done. I think you can go ahead and do the wrong thing for the rest of the day."

I snorted and followed him through the lingering crowd. I wasn't about to tell him I was going to be doing the wrong thing until the pain in my chest faded...which was undoubtedly going to take more than a single day.

It might take forever.

Chapter 4

Langley

'm so glad you're alive, Iker.

Nine months of worry and fear and wishing for things that could never be, and that was what had come out of my mouth when faced with a very real, very present, very gorgeous, Iker Alvarez.

It was the truth. I was so relieved to see him alive and what appeared to be uninjured. He'd looked whole and healthy and so damned beautiful, I'd nearly fallen on my freaking face when our eyes met. His skin held a deeper tan, and his frame looked a little more filled out, like he'd spent whatever downtime he'd had at the gym, but his eyes—those deep brown eyes—were exactly the same. Dark, unreadable, probing. They appeared even more intense and intimidating than the last time I saw them since his face had thinned out, sharpened.

They still saw straight through me.

Right past the manicured hands and salon-perfect hair to the imperfect mess I was on the inside. Those eyes sliced through the bullshit and pretense, and left me flayed open, just like they had nine months ago. Two, maybe three, minutes in his presence and all the work I'd put into healing myself and moving on hadn't mattered.

I was back in that hotel room, under him, feeling that undeniable rush of love flooding my system as he asked me if I was sure. I was kissing him at laser tag. I was curled up on my mother's swing, showing him the best parts of my life since he'd already been exposed to the ugliest.

Nine fucking months of pulling myself together and he undid it all with four words. *I'm so sorry, Langley.*

Langley.

"Langley?" This time, the deep voice was punctuated by a light touch on my wrist.

I blinked, coming out of my Iker-induced stupor to see every set of eyes at the table was on me.

"You okay?" Sam asked, his fingers gentle as always.

"Yes, of course," I replied with a practiced smile. Sam didn't know me well enough to know it was forced. Faked.

Iker did, which was pretty damned ironic, since I'd only spent about a week of my life with him, and I'd already known Sam for a month. Or even longer, I guessed.

Dad's eyebrows rose, as did his glass of champagne. Right. He must have been in the middle of toasting. My fingers curled around my own glass, and I nodded. He smiled, but I knew that his, just like mine, was a smidgen forced.

"I'm so grateful that you could all be here to celebrate Langley tonight." I glanced down the linen tablecloth-covered expanse of the Michelin star-rated restaurant table and nodded to those I recognized. I sat at the foot of the table, the mirror to where my father sat at the head, flanked by Virginia on his right and Camille on his left. Richard occupied the seat next to his pregnant wife, and the eight or so other guests were friends or business acquaintances of my father, until I got to Sam, who sat calmly on my right.

"It's no secret that I'm incredibly proud of both of my daughters," he said, offering Camille a soft smile. "But tonight, I'm especially proud of all that Langley has achieved. She's never backed down from a challenge, has conquered every obstacle with what I know is her mother's grace, what I hope is my tenacity. And yet, she has grown up to be more than all we could've hoped for. So, I ask that you raise your glass to Langley in congratulations. I can't wait to see you take on the world." He lifted his glass to his eye level. "To Langley."

Everyone at the table raised their glasses. "To Langley," they repeated.

I lifted my glass to my lips and took a sip of the sweet champagne, and though I knew Dad had made special arrangements to be sure this was my favorite, it didn't taste as light or as sweet as usual. Because as I looked down the table, and its fourteen occupants, I knew only one of them genuinely loved me. The rest of them were here only for personal gain. Whether it was my father's favor, his backing in a new business, or even access to me, they all wanted something.

And in that moment, I only wanted Iker.

"You sure you're okay?" Sam asked quietly. His eyes were kind and at odds with his rugged and rough appearance. It was what had attracted me to him when we crossed paths in our shared apartment building.

"Yeah," I answered with a small nod, voice obviously strained. "It's just been a big day."

"I bet. It just seems like you've been off since those two guys showed up at the graduation ceremony." He left the space open for me to elaborate, to explain Iker and Gael's presence.

It was odd, because though I wasn't close to Sam, I'd also never hidden anything from him. We'd gone out a few times, enjoyed a casual date or two, but I didn't want to tell him about my surprise guests. Even though every other occupant at the table had met Iker at Camille and Richard's wedding, he felt like something entirely and completely private. Not in the way that secrets were private, but the way memories and small treasures were.

Iker was mine. No one had ever affected me the way he had. No one had ever effortlessly made me feel so special and cherished.

"Really, I'm fine," I assured him. "It's just odd to think that four years of hard work is finally over."

"I get that," he said with a smile as dessert was served.

I reveled in the satisfying crack of my spoon through the crystallized shell of the crème brûlée, then paused before even lifting the first bite. Was I seriously more excited about my dessert than the fact that Sam was here?

Yes. And that was a problem.

Who was I kidding? I knew exactly what the real problem was. *Who* my problem was.

"Langley," Camille called from down the table. When my eyes lifted to hers, she continued with a raised eyebrow. "Daddy just said that he saw Iker at graduation?"

So much for keeping private the fact my world was once again off its axis.

"Yes. He stopped by with his little brother." I shoved my dessert in my mouth in hopes the questioning would end there.

"So, he's back?" she pushed.

"It would appear so," I answered, and ignored the questioning look Sam gave me.

"So, are you..." Her gaze flickered between Sam and me.

"The crème brûlée is delicious, Dad," I blurted, then quickly turned all of my focus to the dish.

"I'm so glad you like it, honey."

I wasn't sure how I made it through the rest of dinner. I knew I made polite conversation, but I felt cleaved in two. While my brain was here, in the restaurant, my stupid, foolish, aching heart was wondering where Iker was now. When had he gotten back? How was he doing? Was his brother taking care of him? What was he doing? Was he dating anyone? Did it even matter?

"You're sure you're okay?" Sam asked as he walked me to the parking lot outside the restaurant. "I know I keep asking, but I can't help but think that you're not."

Before I could answer, I heard Camille call my name, and turned to see her coming toward me.

"Give me a second?" I asked Sam.

"Of course," he replied. "I'll start the car."

Camille looked over my shoulder as she approached. "What are you going to do?"

"About what?" I wrapped my arms around my middle to ward off the May breeze. I loved this little white lace skater dress, but it didn't exactly protect me from a Colorado evening.

"Are you serious?" Camille blatantly rolled her eyes at me.

"We're not talking about Iker." Not now. Not ever.

She cocked an eyebrow at me. "Fine. You don't have to talk about the smoking hot soldier. I will, instead. I know you're not fine. You were still a miserable mess when I got back from my honeymoon, and he'd only been gone for nearly a month then."

"Why do you even care, Camille?" While we weren't at each other's throats like we had been in the past, we also weren't friends. I'd also made my peace with the fact we would never be sisters. Not really.

"I don't," she protested, then sighed, rubbing the skin between her eyebrows. "Okay, that's a lie. I do care a little. I'm really happy. You should get to be happy, and dating Mr. Iker-light over there with the burly beard isn't making you happy."

"I'm happy," I argued. What could she possibly know about my happiness, other than how to destroy it?

She shook her head at me, then pulled her phone from her purse and scrolled until she found what she was looking for. "Here." She turned her phone so I could see the screen.

My heart slammed to life in my chest as I saw Iker dancing with me at her wedding. His arms were around my waist, and mine his neck, and though we danced on a crowded floor, we looked at each other as if we were the only ones in the universe.

I tore my eyes away from the photo. I'd avoided looking at all of her wedding pictures for this exact reason. Pain cut me to the quick, not because of that moment, but as a warning to protect myself from what had followed.

"This is happy," she said softly. "That"—she motioned behind me, where I heard Sam start the car—"is making do. There's a big difference."

"You're right," I agreed coolly. "Happy gets your heart broken. Let's not forget the man who makes you so happy did so at my expense. I'm not up for a repeat."

I walked away from my stepsister and climbed into Sam's SUV. The big electrician drove me home wrapped in a cocoon of heavy silence, as if sensing whatever possibility we'd once had, had died a swift and sudden death.

"Thank you for coming tonight," I told him as he pulled up to our building. "And for being there for me today."

"Of course. Do you want me to walk you up? Not that it's a sketchy area of town or anything," he half-heartedly teased with a tilt to his smile. He lived a few floors lower than I did in the complex, so the offer was sweet but overkill.

"Not tonight. I'll call you?" My hand was already on the door. If that wasn't a metaphor for what was going on here, I didn't know what was.

"I'll answer," he said.

I gave him a nod, then got out of the car and shut the door. I didn't look back as I walked into my building. I took the elevator to the fifth floor. Normally, I would've taken the stairs, but all day in my favorite heels left my feet aching. I fished through my clutch to get to my keys as the elevator doors opened, and didn't look up until I was already halfway down the hall. When I did, I stopped dead in my tracks.

A man sat, leaning with his back against my door, his knees raised to his chest. Black hair escaped in the spaces between his fingers as he cradled his head, his elbows resting on his knees. I didn't need him to look up to know it was Iker. Gone was the polite button-up shirt he'd worn to graduation. Now, he wore a gray Henley with pushed-up sleeves, exposing the ink on his arms. A memory flashed of the last time I'd had those arms around me, and I quickly shoved it away.

"What are you doing here?" I asked him, my voice coming out soft instead of the harsh snap I'd been hoping for.

His gaze jerked to mine, and his eyes, wide and bloodshot, still felt like a punch to the stomach. "Langley," he said with a soft slur as he clambered to his feet. "I was waiting for you."

No, you weren't. You left me without a word so that neither one of us could wait for the other. The bitter thought burned and left a sour taste in my mouth.

"Why? How did you even know where I live?" I knew the answer before the question even left my mouth, and shook my head. "Gael. He asked for my address so he could keep me updated on his progress at school."

Iker raked his hand through his hair, the dark locks still looked soft and silky. "Don't be mad. He's a good kid. Just trying to help his brother out."

He stepped closer and my eyes drifted up. I'd almost forgotten how tall he was. How his size dwarfed mine and made me feel so very delicate.

Breakable.

"Are you drunk?" I answered in challenge.

40

"Maybe." He smiled, and my chest constricted. "Are you mad?"

"Maybe." The truth was, I didn't know what I was. "Probably."

Standing this close to him, catching the combined scents of alcohol, his cologne, and the peppermints he loved, had me struggling to remember exactly *when* we were. All the time and space between us was so easy to forget when he was this close. This vital and alive. This real. "Why are you here?"

"I wanted— I needed to see you." He tucked his thumbs in the front pockets of his ripped jeans and I gripped my clutch and keys so hard they bit into the thin skin of my palms. The motion tugged the denim down low on his lean hips and exposed a hint of his insanely chiseled, and artfully tattooed, abs.

It would be so easy to cross the inches that separated us. To rise on my toes, even higher than the heels I wore, and brush my lips against his. My body hummed with awareness at his nearness. I hadn't been with anyone since him, but I doubted he could say the same. I wasn't stupid. I'd been the less experienced one of the two of us, and I highly doubted the week he'd no doubt found inconsequential had done much to slow his rate of conquest. Guys like him didn't change.

Girls like me didn't either...we were always going to have a soft spot for our first blinding, all-consuming, stupid first love.

"God, Langley, I'm so sorry. So fucking sorry." He stepped toward me and I retreated.

"You said that. You know what you didn't say? Goodbye." It would have made all the difference.

In my dreams, I'll still be in that bed with you. The words from his letter hit me like a freight train, like they always did when I thought about him. How many times had I read that damn thing? Enough that the creases were soft from handling and the words were blurred from my fingers, yet crisp in my mind.

"I know. I should have. I didn't know how to tell you. How to leave you." He took another step and I retreated again. I couldn't chance him touching me. Apparently, the chemistry I thought I'd imagined was very real, and I couldn't afford to let it overpower my common sense. It was weird how the things I thought were real, and the ones I'd convinced myself weren't, had blurred together with time.

"That's funny, considering you managed to leave just fine."

His eyes sparked, and I knew I'd hit a nerve. "You're right, I did. But I'm standing here right now. Don't you feel anything?"

Anger whipped through me, and this time, it was me stepping forward and him retreating. "Feel anything? Do I feel anything? Are you kidding me?" I felt so much. Too much. It was practically choking me.

"Langley," he pleaded, putting his hands out like he was under arrest, but the fire still raged in his eyes.

"You have the nerve to show up at my graduation nine months after sneaking out of my bed, leaving me like a cheap, discarded rental tux, and then ask if I still feel anything?"

You don't belong in my world any more than I belong in yours. Yours would suffocate me, and mine would ruin you. Ruin and suffocation. That was how he saw us.

"Hey, it looks like you were feeling things just fine with Beard-O at graduation," he snapped.

What the hell? Was the guy who had zero use for me actually jealous? He had no right to be. Not when he was the one who'd walked away, who hadn't given me a chance to so much as wait for him. I hadn't even been worthy of fucking waiting.

"I feel plenty, Iker." His back hit the wall next to my door, and I brought my body against his, blocking out every nerve that fired in absolute anticipation. I might have been pissed as hell at him, but my body remembered all too well what he could do, and was more than ready for an encore.

Shit. My sex drive hadn't been off because of school, or stress, or anything else. It had gone dormant because I only wanted Iker.

Fuck my life. Fuck him and his stupid, smoldering sex appeal, perfect face, and amazing body. I wanted to hate him so badly, and instead hated myself because no matter how hard I tried to force it, I never managed to get all the way there.

"Really? What exactly is plenty?" he asked, his gaze dropping to my lips before wetting his own.

Hell no. I wasn't falling into this trap again. Wasn't handing myself over on a platter to have him tell me I wasn't what he wanted or needed. He had no faith in me. He honestly believed I couldn't survive his lifestyle and made it clear he blatantly hated mine. He didn't get to be the one who decided what I could and couldn't handle. He didn't get to make me feel like I wasn't good enough, or strong enough. I understood, I deserved more...he was the one who taught me that much-needed lesson.

"I fell for you," I whispered, letting my fists rest against his chest, keeping my clutch and keys between us like a barrier.

His eyes flew wide, but I didn't let myself stop to examine whatever emotion could be there. I couldn't afford to care.

"It took me one week to fall in love with you. It took me every single month that you've been gone to recover when you walked out. So, yeah, I feel plenty. But mostly"—I stepped back, my skin cooling immediately from the lack of his body heat—"I just feel over you. I feel like whatever we had, whatever we may have been, is gone."

He didn't need to know there was no putting my heart back together when he left. He never needed to know he took the stupid thing with him when he walked out the door.

The words trailed off, softer than I wanted them to be, but I stiffened my spine, refusing to be moved by the way he almost completely deflated in front of me. His dark eyes went downcast and his wide shoulders slumped. I took the opportunity to move around him, but I should've known better.

A predator was even more dangerous when injured.

Chapter 5

Iker

There was fear in Langley's eyes.

I recognized it clearly because it was the same expression she wore the night I saved her from a group of rowdy drunks outside a dive bar she had no business being in. Her blue eyes were twice their normal size, and she looked like she was ready to chew a hole through her bottom lip. Her entire body flinched when I reached out to grab her arm as she tried to slide around me. I heard her suck in a sharp breath and immediately let my hand fall without it touching her. I understood her anger and resentment, even through the fine haze of alcohol-driven bravery that brought me to her door. I could handle those feelings, but not the fear.

I desperately wanted to believe she knew me well enough, even though we only spent a week together, to understand I would rather die than cause her any harm. Sighing, I shifted my weight, watching as she purposely put more space between us, now that it was clear I wasn't going to touch her or force her to do anything.

Gael tried to tell me approaching her after I'd spent the afternoon trying to drink her memory away was a terrible idea. I should've listened to the kid. After all, he was the smartest person I'd ever met. However, I couldn't shake the image of her wrapped up in the bearded guy's arms. I couldn't forget the surprise and relief on her too-pretty face when she finally caught sight of me. I couldn't convince myself to walk away again, even if it was what would be best for both of us.

"Langley." She paused, keys in the door as she looked over her shoulder in my direction. I could hear the desperation and pleading in my own voice. I'd never sounded so close to an emotional breaking point.

Slowly, she turned to face me and I closed the distance between us. I didn't touch her, but I stepped into her personal space, crowding her back against the still-locked apartment door. I braced a hand above her head and leaned down so we were eye to eye. Her breath caught and my blood burned as she lifted her palms to my chest and unsuccessfully tried to push me back. I felt her shiver, and it killed me not knowing if the reaction was spurred by fear or something else. She used to quiver whenever I was close because we were both fighting an attraction that was bigger than both of us. We couldn't help but react to one another, or the urge to reach out and touch whenever we could.

"I broke this. Now, I'm going to be the one to fix it." A bold claim for sure, but I felt helpless to do anything else. I honestly felt like I couldn't breathe under the weight of being so close to her, yet so far away. She'd fallen in love with me, but didn't feel that way anymore.

Langley scoffed and her hands fell away. She blinked her bright eyes as her golden eyebrows dipped down in a fierce frown. "You didn't break it. You destroyed it. You took it away and smashed it into a million pieces, and didn't give me a chance to save it or put it back together. There is no fixing *it*. You need to leave, Iker. You're drunk, and we're finished." She tried to push me away again, but I leaned closer.

I let the tip of my nose brush across her soft cheek, and inhaled her sweet, summery scent before allowing her to force me backward. I stumbled a step, shoving my hands in the front pocket of my jeans as Langley let out a relieved breath and turned to disappear into her apartment.

Swearing under my breath, knowing good and well my surprise visit had hurt my case more than helped, I started to make my way back down to the parking lot so I could call an Uber and get a ride back to my own place. I was brought up short when a dark image separated from the other shadows surrounding the entrance to the stairwell. The big guy with the beard didn't look any happier to see me than Langley did. His burly arms were crossed over his broad chest, and the glare on his face would've been enough to intimidate another man. I was too buzzed and caught up in my own emotional downward spiral to feel the obvious threat emanating from him.

I lifted an eyebrow as he took a step in my direction. "Just leave her alone. She's finally starting to put herself first and focus on her future. You have no right to show up out of the blue and undo all the work she put into putting herself back together after you left. She's better off without you."

He wasn't saying anything I hadn't told myself a hundred times, but hearing it from a stranger, from a man who was free to touch and comfort the only girl I'd ever managed to care about, pissed me off and poked at a soft spot I didn't even know I'd developed. I'd never been a particularly good guy, but I'd also never really been a bad guy either. I hated playing the role of the villain in any story Langley was telling about us.

"She's better off with you, right?" The words came out on a growl. I took my hands out of my pockets and scowled as they automatically curled into fists.

The guy with the beard shook his head and returned my fierce look. "I've been into her for a long time. If she'd give me half a chance, I would never let her go. But, she's scared. Every time she gives her heart to someone, they let her go and leave her behind. She's not willing to part with it anymore. She's too afraid of being hurt again, of trusting anyone fully."

The words hit harder than his fists ever would. I lifted a hand to the spot in the center of my chest that wouldn't stop aching.

"It's better for everyone if you don't show up again. Langley is slowly healing; she has a lot lined up in the next few weeks as she plans for her future. She doesn't need to be distracted, or tormented, by you." He sighed and lifted a hand to stroke his beard. "Just leave her alone."

I'd planned on doing that very thing...until I saw her. As soon as I caught sight of her glimmering, golden hair, and her genuine, joyful smile, I knew there was no way I could pretend I wasn't still hung up on the girl who would always be way out of my league.

Grunting in response, I shifted around the competition, carefully maneuvering my way to the stairs. It'd be much harder to try and win Langley back if I was laid up in the hospital with a bunch of broken bones.

"I don't think I can do that, bud." I wasn't about to become a stalker, but I knew the pain in my heart, the ache filling my chest, wouldn't stop throbbing unless I tried my best to right all the wrongs I'd tossed in Langley's lap. "I walked away once, and it was the stupidest decision I ever made."

The bearded guy shook his shaggy head and sighed heavily. "She's never going to give you another chance to break her heart."

I shrugged and turned my back on him. "That's okay."

I didn't need a chance to break it. I'd already been there and done that. I needed a second chance so she could hopefully forgive me and give me a shot to undo all the damage I'd done. She might never let herself love me again because she felt the risk was too high. I deserved that, I really did. But, I couldn't shake the feeling I needed to do my best, to do *something* in order to smooth over some of the jagged pieces I'd left behind when I forcibly ripped myself out of her life.

Maybe if I could show her I was a good guy who made a bad choice, we could both start over. I had a feeling her forgiveness would be the thing that set us both free.

"You'll have to go through me to get to her." It was an obvious warning, but instead of making me mad, the harsh words were reassuring. The guy obviously cared about Langley a lot. And while I hated he got to touch her, kiss her, hold her, when she wouldn't even let me get close, I appreciated that he was willing to stand between her and whatever—or whoever—was trying to hurt her. She deserved nothing less.

I shot a loose wave over my shoulder to indicate I heard the challenge clearly, then proceeded to jog down the steps. By the time I hit the parking lot, a good chunk of my buzz was gone and my fuzzy mind was starting to work a little quicker. Langley told me to back off, and I had to respect her wishes. I was actually pretty proud of her for speaking her mind, instead of hiding behind the icy politeness she used when dealing with someone in the wrong from her very-privileged life.

Somewhere along the line she'd learned how to advocate for herself, and I owed it to her to respect the boundaries she'd put in place. That didn't mean I was ready to turn tail and give up. No, I'd just have to be more careful about how I tried to get a foot in the door she'd firmly shut in my face.

My Uber driver was an older guy who immediately pegged me as a soldier. The short ride was filled with him asking me all about the current state of the military and grilling me on my thoughts about the political climate we were currently serving in. I tried to keep my answers short and sweet since I was in no shape to carry my half of the debate. By the time I got to my apartment, I was exhausted and felt turned inside out.

Gael was stretched out on the couch, watching reruns of *Bob's Burgers*. He immediately turned the TV off and got to his feet when I stumbled in the door.

"I was wondering if I was going to have to come bail you out of jail since you were gone for so long. Then I wondered if maybe you and Langley made up." He cocked his head to the side and frowned. "I can tell by your frown that the latter was just wishful thinking."

I shrugged and stomped to the kitchen so I could fish another beer out of the fridge.

"She told me to get lost. Then the guy she's seeing let me know, without question, that he's willing to do whatever it takes to keep her...and keep me away from her." I sighed and rolled the cool can against my forehead. "She was scared of me." My voice faded out on a whisper as Gael watched me with concern clear in his gaze.

"So, what are you going to do now? Is this it?" He sounded as disappointed as I felt.

Slowly, I shook my head. "No. This is just the beginning." I cracked open the beer and took a giant swig. I dragged the back of my hand across my mouth and lifted my eyebrows. "Now, I get creative and try to win her over without crowding her."

I was going to have to try and woo her in the way she was used to. I was going to have to play by a bunch of rules I didn't really understand. Getting her to give me another chance meant putting my pride and ego aside, and doing whatever it took to get her to look at me the way she did when we first met.

Like I was her hero.

Like I was the only one who deserved her real smile and sweet kisses.

She believed I hated the world where she came from, and she wasn't wrong. If I wanted her forever, I was going to have to learn to make peace with all our obvious differences. I was going to have to show her I was making an effort to meet her halfway so we weren't existing in her world or mine. We needed a place in the middle that was just the two of us...our own little world where we could finally be happy.

My baby brother reached out a hand and clapped it on my shoulder. "So, what's the plan?"

I snorted. "Haven't figured that out yet." I didn't have the first clue how to *woo* anyone, let alone someone who was used to the very best.

Gael squeezed my shoulder and gave me a lopsided grin. "Good thing I'm pretty much a genius. I'll help you out."

I snorted out a surprised laugh. "Oh, yeah?"

Gael nodded, face going solemn. "You deserve to be happy, and that girl makes you happy."

She did. She also made me hurt, which wasn't necessarily a bad thing. It made sense that love had to be painful sometimes, or else we wouldn't be able to feel it. We would slowly forget it was there. The pain was a good reminder of what happened when love wasn't taken care of and taken for granted.

I really wanted Langley to forgive me for leaving and for being less than honest with her, but I wondered if I could ever forgive myself for making her hurt the same way I was hurting now.

Chapter 6

Langley

I laid back on my couch and wiggled to get comfortable. Then I opened up Netflix and scanned through the millions of hours of programming I'd been too busy to watch over the last four years.

Today was the first day in my memory that I didn't have something to study for. There was no summer reading list from professors. No lurking deadline for a research paper. No notes to pour over or schedule to plan. I was totally free until I moved for my new job, and now I had zero idea what to do with myself.

I'd already gone for a run. Already showered. Breakfast was made and cleaned up. Chocolate chip cookies were warm on the plate, and popcorn was buttered and salty in the bowl. And I still couldn't relax. I switched positions for the hundredth time, and kept scrolling.

Romantic comedy? Nope. It would just make me think of Iker, which I wasn't about to let happen. Nope. Not thinking of Iker ever again, especially not after he'd shown up drunk and... Iker. Great, now I was using his name as an adjective. Awesome.

Military drama? Way too much Iker. What had a nine-month deployment changed about him? Anything? I'd read tons about soldiers who came home completely different people than when they left, but that was usually due to trauma.

Not sure what part of *I broke this. Now, I'm going to be the one to fix it*, stemmed from war, or alcohol, or regret, or just a desire to fuck with me because he knew he could.

And you told him you'd loved him, you idiot.

I groaned, letting my head fall back on the leather armrest.

Wedding movies? What the hell was Netflix trying to do? Break my heart all over again? I kept scrolling and paused on a horror flick.

Screaming girls running through the woods from a masked serial killer? Bring it on. I flipped around again, wondering when the hell my couch had gotten so uncomfortable, and hit play on the first slasher flick that came up.

Then I sat and waited for it to buffer, cursing the included-in-the-rent, slow Internet in my building.

I could do with a good scare.

Unlike last night, where the only thing I'd been afraid of had been Iker's nearness. He took hold of my arm, and I'd been instantly desperate to get the hell away from him. That man touched me, and my brain stopped working, while the rest of me went into overdrive. If seeing him brought me to my knees, what would happen if he actually got his hands on me?

The thought was completely, utterly terrifying. It had taken me months to rebuild myself when I crumbled after he left. Months until I could make it through most of the day without wondering how he was or if he was safe. What if he unraveled everything I'd struggled to recover with a single touch?

That would be the real horror story.

I flipped around again, then groaned in frustration. Having nothing on my agenda was supposed to be relaxing, refreshing, even. Instead, all it did was give me time to think about the one person I had no business thinking about.

"Screw this." I got off my couch and headed for my bedroom, only to pause when there was a knock at the door.

I opened it as far as the security chain would allow, and immediately my jaw dropped.

"Langley Vaughn?" the delivery guy asked, juggling an iPad and the most beautiful arrangement of calla lilies I'd ever seen.

"Yes?" I answered.

"Sign here, please." He handed me the iPad and I signed the box with the attached stylus after unlocking and fully opening the door. Who on Earth would have sent me those?

"Here you go. Have a nice day." He thrust the square-vase bouquet into my hands and walked back down the hall.

"Thank you!" I called after him, then shut my door with my hip. "Holy shit," I muttered. There had to be two dozen calla lilies here. Whoever sent them had to have spent a small fortune. Dad, maybe? Definitely not Virginia.

I set the lilies on the counter and plucked the small envelope from its clear, forked stand. My heart clenched as I read the note on the card.

Langley,

These reminded me of you—elegant, classy, and beautiful.

I meant what I said last night.

Iker

I read the card twice, then put it on the counter, only to grab it and read it yet again. What he said last night? The part about fixing *it?* Which I assumed meant *us*. That wasn't possible since there wasn't an *us* to fix. Maybe he meant the part about being sorry? About needing to see me?

I put the card down again. No. I wasn't falling for this. I wasn't softening because he sent some flowers. Flowers didn't make up for leaving me in that hotel room with a note and a broken heart. Flowers didn't make up for the highhanded way he'd simply decided I wouldn't be allowed to wait for him.

But those flowers...they were beautiful. Classic and understated, all the more exquisite for their simplicity. They were exactly what I would have picked for myself.

This arrangement was also way out of his price range. This was probably a couple of hundred dollars sitting on my counter, and while they were stunning, he couldn't afford to make gestures like this. That pressure in my chest was back, and I found myself running a finger down the petal.

He shouldn't have, and not just because I was pissed at him, but because they were too much. I didn't need lilies—or even daisies. I'd never been impressed with lavish gifts because I'd grown up in a society where things like this beautiful bouquet were commonplace. But the very reason the flowers frustrated me was the same one that had my stupid heart fluttering.

This wasn't some afterthought by a Broadmoor frat boy.

Iker had sacrificed for these.

That was why I pulled out my phone and clicked on his name to open the text thread I hadn't had the heart to delete nine months ago. I almost didn't send a new message when the unanswered one from the day he deployed stared back at me mockingly. After an inner battle, my long-ingrained manners won out over my hurt feelings and uncertain heart.

Langley: Thank you for the flowers. They're truly breathtaking.

I hit enter before I could think better of it, then watched the dots blink as he responded. This was a mistake, opening a line of communication, but I would have been the world's biggest bitch not to thank him.

Iker: I'm glad you like them. I meant it last night. I'm going to fix what I broke.

I sat on my barstool, and stared at the gorgeous flowers that contrasted with the ugly way he'd left. That fluttering in my heart would only get stronger when it came to him. Hell, it had only taken me a week to fall head over heels for him the first time, and then he'd crushed me. What would happen this time if I let him in, gave him the chance to resurrect the heart he'd eviscerated? I wasn't sure I'd ever recover.

Langley: Please don't. You need to stop.

He left me on read for a hot minute, and I angrily decided I had to follow it up.

Langley: I lost too much last time.

The dots started jumping around as he was typing out a response.

Iker: You weren't the only one who lost.

I sucked in a breath. His pain had been evident in that letter, but so had his unwillingness to try. I hadn't been worth the effort of the two of us figuring things out together.

I wasn't worth that effort to *anyone* I'd ever been close to. Not here, at least. Maybe Texas would be different. I could start fresh and focus on myself.

Langley: I wasn't the one who walked out. Thank you again, the flowers are spectacular, and I know they must have cost you a fortune, but you can't fix what doesn't exist.

Iker: Watch me.

I spent the next day volunteering at my favorite no-kill animal shelter. There was zero point to sitting around binge-watching fourteen seasons of *Grey's Anatomy* when I could be out helping someone who needed it.

Besides, soothing someone else's misery helped take the focus off my own. Sam had texted that morning, just to check in on me, and I hadn't responded. Maybe it was because I was realizing I wasn't nearly as invested as he was. Maybe it was because of the flowers Iker sent yesterday. Either way, I was going to have to make some choices. But not right now.

I walked all the pups I could and snuck in some extra time with Einstein, a mutt with a shock of white hair and more personality than most people. He'd been at the shelter a week, and had won me over instantly.

After ruffling his soft, fluffy fur one last time, I put him back in his kennel and tried to steel myself against his whines as I walked away. There were so many little souls here in need of homes.

"Any nibbles on Einstein?" I asked the girl at the desk.

"Not yet," she answered, barely looking up from her screen. There was just so much to do and not many of us to share the load.

I posted his pic on my Instagram before I left, and added his details, but most of the people who followed me weren't the adoption type. They were the perfectly bred, AKC-certified, show-dog type.

I'd just gotten home when the doorbell rang again.

This time, the delivery girl had me sign on a piece of paper, and I had a sneaking suspicion who my benefactor was. I thanked her, shut the door, and opened the wide, flat box.

Chocolate-dipped strawberries spelled out, "I'm sorry."

The note read:

Langley,
They're almost as sweet as you taste.
I'm never giving up.
Iker

"Ugh!" I groaned, slapping the card onto my counter. Then I ate one of the strawberries, but only because I was hungry, and they looked—holy shit, they were good. So good.

Almost as decadent as kissing Iker had been. Sweet and silky, passionate and abandoned, stealing my inhibitions and turning me into someone I didn't recognize by simply placing zero expectations on me.

I knew it was another mistake, but my mom would have raised a disappointed eyebrow if I didn't say thank you.

Langley: Thank you for the strawberries. They're wonderful. Now stop.

That was stern enough, right? This couldn't go on. It just couldn't.

Iker: They reminded me of kissing you.

I paused mid-bite, my lips wrapped around one of the berries. I somehow barely managed to chew and swallow around the lump that popped into my throat. A shiver danced down my spine. As different as we were, we'd always managed to be on the same wavelength. Sometimes he seemed to know exactly what I was thinking without me saying a word, or even being in the same room.

Langley: The strawberries looked good, but they're nothing compared to your mouth.

Iker: The chocolate is the dark stuff, a little bitter, but it just brings out how sweet the strawberries really are. They complement each other. Like you and me.

Oh God, now all I could think about was kissing him. I missed kissing him. Missed touching him. Laughing with him.

Langley: You have to stop spending your money on me.

Iker: No.

Langley: It's not getting you anywhere.

Okay, that was a lie, because I sat there and watched those blinking dots like they were my lifeline.

Iker: It got me this text message. Well worth any amount of money.

I laughed, and shook my head.

The next day, he sent a gift certificate to the Broadmoor Spa, with a note that told me if he couldn't put his hands on me, then an expert should get the honor. Considering I'd spent three of my days with him at the Broadmoor, it was bittersweet, but I melted at the nod to the fact he wasn't shying away from our past.

I spent the next morning at the shelter, walking the pups and snuggling Einstein, and then I took advantage of that spa massage.

I texted a picture of my fluffy slippers as I waited to be pampered.

Iker: I envy your shoes. What does that say about how desperate I am?

You'd just use them to walk out on me again. My thought was instant, but my response wasn't.

Langley: Admit it, you miss the Broadmoor, even with all the snobbery.

It was the closest to teasing I'd gotten with him, even if it held a note of the truth. Even if he was sorry, and I did give him a chance, what was it good for? He hated the world I lived in, and flat-out said I couldn't handle his. Plus, I was moving soon, so why put us through it?

Iker: I miss you. And I'd happily put on a damned tie if it meant I could be near you.

He didn't need a tie. I didn't need the Broadmoor, or his sweet, over-the-top gestures. I'd needed him, and that painful ache in my heart told me maybe I still did.

The next day, he sent me a crate of pineapples. An. Entire. Crate. The note had been an address. I was guessing his. I shook my head at the fruit, and then flat-out lost it, laughing like a mad woman. What was I supposed to do with all this? And why wasn't I as mad as I should have been? Frustrated? Yes. Confused? You bet.

I hefted the crate into my arms and headed for the car. Pineapples buckled into the passenger seat, I popped the address into the GPS and headed where the British woman in my car's system told me to go.

Fifteen minutes later, I found myself outside an apartment complex south of downtown and close to Fort Carson. It wasn't too far from the dive bar I'd met him at, which had only been a couple of miles from my dad's.

I'd lived so close to Iker and never known it for all the years he'd been in the Springs.

Pineapples hefted on my hip, I climbed the stairs to the third floor, then knocked on the door that corresponded with the address.

A minute later, the door opened, revealing a very surprised, very casual Iker.

His hair was military-short at the sides, but the top looked ruffled, like he'd just gotten out of bed. His jeans were his typical dark, ripped-up ones that made me want to ask him to turn around just so I could watch him walk away, and his T-shirt was gray and stretched tight across muscles that hadn't been as big when he'd left Colorado, and his tattoos rippled when his hands flexed on the doorframe. I hated how good he looked almost as much as I hated my reaction to it.

That warmth in my belly sure as hell wasn't anger.

"Seriously?" I asked, then pushed my way past him to walk into his apartment. It was neat, but screamed his bachelor status. Funny the only thing he left a mess was *me*.

"Hey, Gael," I said with a smile as I put the crate of pineapples on the sturdy, bar-height kitchen table.

"Langley," he said slowly from the couch, his eyes flying toward his brother.

"You're here," Iker said, just as slowly.

"You sent me a crate of tropical fruit, and your address. What else was I supposed to do?"

His eyes did a fast sweep of my body, and that warmth only spiked hotter. Suddenly, I wished I'd taken more time than my cut-off jeans and pink tank showed. Shit, I hadn't thought about makeup or my hair, which was piled on my head in a knot to keep it from sticking to my neck when walking the dogs.

"I did send you the pineapples." His gaze cut to Gael. "But the address?"

Gael shuffled to his feet with an overly innocent smile. "You know what? I think I'm going to get some fresh air on a walk to...well, anywhere that isn't here." He slapped Iker's chest on his way out the door. "You're welcome, big bro. Langley, his actual note is written on a notebook by my seat, if you're curious." He left the living room with a wink, leaving me ten feet away from Iker.

We stood there, staring at each other, the tension building until I was afraid one of us might snap. "Don't be mad at him. He's a good kid," I said with a shaky smile, using his own words against him.

His eyes flared in surprise, and then he smiled. God, I'd missed that smile. They were rare and always had to be earned. "How can I be mad when he got me exactly what I wanted?"

Okay, now that made me melt.

"You have to stop sending me stuff," I chided, but it didn't come out as harsh as I wanted.

"These remind me of you because they look all prickly, but they're sweet once you get under the skin. That's what the note was supposed to say."

"Well..." I huffed. "I don't have a good, snarky response for that." I folded my arms under my breasts. "You look bigger, by the way." *Oh, shoot me now.* I cringed. "Not that you were small before. And not that I was looking... Just an observation."

Great, now he was flat-out grinning, those straight, even teeth catching part of his lower lip and making me wet my own subconsciously. His grin faded when he saw me do it. "When you're deployed, you get a lot of downtime on days when you're not running missions. I spent my free time working out and thinking." He moved toward me slowly, but didn't crowd me.

"What did you think about?" I asked as he opened a drawer in the desk that sat across from the table.

"My family," he answered, pulling out an envelope, and turning to lean against the desk. I was incredibly grateful for the space, even as I debated crossing it. "And you."

I swallowed as heat flushed my face. "I thought that thinking about me was the reason you didn't want to be together while you were deployed? You said I'd be too much of a distraction, right?" My voice was soft, even if the words grated.

The envelope in his hand crinkled as his grip tightened on it. "You have no idea how many times I wish I'd done things differently. But then we lost two guys in Alpha Company and I couldn't help but think that I did the right thing by you. Because, what if I was next?"

Anger. Sadness. Regret. It all slammed into me from so many directions, I didn't know what to feel. "I'm sorry your fellow soldiers died. Were you friends?" I couldn't imagine waking up and not knowing if you'd live through the day, if the people you cared about would.

"Not friends, but I knew them. And thanks." He looked away, and I couldn't help but wonder if he was still the guy I'd fallen for, and if not, what parts had changed? "Do you get it? Why I didn't want that for you?"

"No," I answered. "You took my choice and made a huge decision for me because you didn't think I was capable of making what you considered to be the right one. You spent that whole week telling me to stand up for myself, to break free of the dictates of the world I come from, and then you turned around and did the dictating and undermining yourself."

He blanched. "I wasn't...that isn't what I..." His hand swept over his face. "God, you tie me in fucking knots. I didn't want you to get hurt. I never wanted to hurt you."

"I was hurt the minute I realized you'd left without a real explanation, much less a kiss goodbye. I worried about you every day," I admitted. "I tried to forget about you, that's true, but you were in my head, even when I wished you weren't." It hadn't mattered that he didn't want me as much as I had wanted him, my heart had just been too stubborn to let go.

"Same here." He moved forward, pushing off the desk. "Look, I fucked up. It won't happen again."

"You're right," I answered, retreating backward until my lower back connected with the table. "It won't."

"Because you won't give me a second chance?" He pushed up in my personal space.

"Iker..." I shook my head, not trusting my mouth.

"Give me a shot, Langley. You won't regret it." His voice slid over me like that damned chocolate over the strawberries—dark, luscious, and sinfully good.

"I already do." He was close enough I could feel the heat of his skin through our clothing. I missed him. I wanted him. If he touched me now, I was going over, and I knew it.

"Are you scared of me now?" he whispered.

"No, not of you. I'm terrified of the way you make me feel." The confession spilled out, and I flinched, knowing I'd just handed him the power.

His hand slowly rose to cup my cheek, and he brushed his thumb over my cheekbone with a mixture of relief and awe on his face. "Yeah, well, you scare the shit out of me too. This?" His hands moved to my hips, and the air swooshed from my lungs. "What happens when I touch you? It doesn't exist anywhere else for me."

He put the envelope on the table and lifted me with an ease that sent jolts of need throughout my body and set me on the table, then stepped between my knees.

I was so royally fucked.

My pulse beat erratically, my breath came fast and harsh, and my traitor of a body went all soft and pliant when it should have locked up with a do-not-enter sign. Instead, my thighs opened wider.

"Give. Me. A. Chance." His demand came with that intense, smoldering look that had stripped me out of my clothes more than once. "Come on, Langley. You know how good we are together."

My willpower teetered on the edge, and he saw it, damn him.

"Look, I know about the boyfriend—"

"I don't have a boyfriend," I blurted, then cursed my lack of control around Iker.

"Beard-O?"

"Oh, Sam? We've seen each other a couple of times, but we're not serious, or exclusive. He's kissed me once, but there's no spark. I very much wish there was fireworks between us for obvious reasons. But, nothing."

His confusion turned into a smirk, and I immediately regretted telling him. "No spark?" His grip tightened and he tugged me forward until our hips met. "I don't think we have that particular problem."

Given the way my blood turned molten and his eyes darkened, I would have agreed with him.

"Attraction was never our problem." It had just created more of them in the long run.

"I was the problem," he retorted. "And now I'm going to be the solution. Ditch the beard and let me take you out. Give me a chance to really date you. To prove I'm invested in you, in what we could have together if we fight for it." He must have seen me waver because something

67

like hope sparked in his eyes and he looked away to grab that envelope he'd ditched a moment earlier. "Here. Take it. It's ten thousand dollars."

My eyebrows hit my hairline. "What?"

"It's the money you paid me for the wedding."

It was only the sheer nervousness on his face that kept me seated. It took every ounce of self-control I possessed not to throw the envelope in his face. "This is money you earned. In a mutually beneficial transaction." Then again, given the number of orgasms he'd given me on top of pissing off my family probably made it a bit more of a benefit to me.

"Money I need you to take back." He stared me down and his jaw twitched.

"No. You paid Gael's tuition with that money. Well, obviously not *that* money, since it's in an envelope. And not a bank. How the hell did you even get ten thousand dollars?" If it had been that easy for him, he wouldn't have needed me in the first place.

"I sublet my apartment while I was gone. Plus, it's not like I had anywhere to spend money while I was deployed. My truck is paid off, so nine months of pay is sitting in my account. I know it's nothing compared—"

I slapped my hand across his mouth, then immediately regretted *that* decision when he scraped his teeth across my palm. Act, regret, act, regret. That seemed to be my pattern with him today. I snatched my hand away and glared at him. "Don't finish that sentence. And I'm not taking your money. You worked for that!"

"I can't keep it. Not knowing that you paid off Gael's tuition—"

68

"You were never supposed to know about that! They promised it would be anonymous!" I took a calming breath. "It wasn't just for you...or Gael."

"I can't have that fucked-up power dynamic between us. So please take it, so I can date you. Please." He put the envelope in my hand.

It was odd how ten thousand dollars from my trust fund felt insanely lighter than ten thousand dollars he'd bled for. It was heavy in my palm, and the plea broke me like a giant with a twig. *Snap.*

"Okay," I whispered.

"Okay?" His eyes widened.

"Okay, I'll go on one date with you. Just one. And it's only on the condition that you stop sending expensive stuff to my place and you never try to give this money back to me ever again." I took the envelope and pushed it against his chest. His very built, very tattooed, very close chest that was only separated from my hand by the thin cotton of his T-shirt. Was there any wonder I couldn't feel a spark with Sam? There was no one on this freaking Earth who lit my fuse and heated me up like Iker.

His jaw ticked again. "One date."

"One date." I nodded.

"You won't take this money." His lips pursed, but his hand covered mine, warm and strong. Hands that knew exactly how I liked to be touched.

"If you ask again, I'm walking out that door, and this offer goes with me. Those are my terms." The logical side of me hissed at my stupidity. The part of me that hummed in his presence practically purred and begged to rub up against him.

"Fine, I accept your terms."

"Good." It was the second deal we'd ever made, but I already knew there was way more riding on this arrangement.

He lowered his head slowly, giving me every opportunity to pull away, but I couldn't. I was powerless against those brown eyes and the way he looked at me like I was equal parts infuriating and enchanting.

I tilted my face up to his and my lips parted, already heavy with the expectation of—

"Hey! Oh, whoa. Bad timing." Gael's voice broke through the haze of arousal, and I shoved at Iker's chest.

"You think?" Iker snapped at his little brother, but he moved at my insistence.

"Nope! It was perfect timing. Really." I poked my head over the crate and pulled my keys out of the fruit where they'd fallen.

"I'll just be going!" I gave Iker a thumbs-up, which was pretty much the most awkward, cringy moment of my life, raced out of his apartment, and nodded to Gael before I pulled the door shut with excessive force.

What the hell had I just done? Hadn't I learned that playing with fire was going to end up leaving my heart burned and turned to ash? What was I thinking, sticking my hands back into the exact same flames that had left wounds I was still trying to keep from becoming scars I couldn't ever get rid of?

Chapter 7

Iker

I tugged at the silk knot of the tie at the base of my throat for what had to be the thousandth time that night. Every time my fingers touched the expensive material, I got a look from Langley. She was usually an open book. I could read whatever it was she might be feeling by looking into her eyes. The blue depths were clear and expressive. Tonight, they were shuttered and cool. I couldn't tell if she was having a good time, or if she would rather be anywhere else instead of sitting across the table from me at this five-star restaurant.

Her gaze lingered on the fabric of the tie as she reached for the glass of red wine on the table in front of her. The awkward silence was almost unbearable. Before I screwed everything up between the two of us, we could talk about anything. Our differing life experiences and wildly opposite upbringing always made for interesting conversation. Because we were so inherently different, it was always a challenge trying to get the other person to see a situation in a new light. Being together forced us to be more open and accepting so we could appreciate all the trials and turmoil the other went through in order to become the person we loved now.

Tonight, none of that easy banter could be found. We were both stiff and formal with one another. Langley barely touched her dinner, and she hadn't seemed overly thrilled with the exhibition on Native American art I'd taken her to before it was time for our reservation. I spent more time than I wanted to admit trying to plan the kind of date I thought she was used to. The kind of date a classy chick like Langley deserved. I needed to prove to her I could step it up and she wouldn't miss out on anything if she agreed to give me a second chance. I wanted the effort I put into making amends to be obvious. I was desperate for her to understand how serious I was about undoing all the damage I'd done.

However, the beautiful blonde sitting across from me seemed far more annoyed than she did impressed. She'd been hesitant from the get-go when I told her what I was planning for our first official date. I figured she simply still had doubts about my sincerity and staying power. She was reluctant to let me get close when I'd already hurt her, and I couldn't blame her for that.

But, it was driving me nuts that she wouldn't tell me what she was thinking, and that I couldn't read if she believed the risk of giving me another shot was worth the reward. I spent the whole night bending over backwards to give her an unforgettable first date, and all I got in return were a few narrow-eyed looks and one-word responses to everything I asked her.

Fighting back the urge to shift nervously in my chair, I ran my palm over the luxurious material of the tie and forced a grin. I knew the moment would make the dimple in my cheek pop out, and for once this evening, I knew exactly what Langley was thinking. She'd been weak for that dimple from the very beginning. Finally, a spark of something bright and lively lit up in her cool, cerulean gaze.

"Now that you're done with school, what are your plans? Are you going to work for your dad?" I still wasn't sure what an economist did, but had no doubt she would kick ass at whatever she chose to do for a living.

Langley shifted in her seat and swirled the wine around in the obviously expensive glass. "He wanted me to work for him, but I picked a different company. I wanted to stand on my own two feet. I also wanted to focus on a company and career path that focuses more on non-profit and charitable investments. No matter what line of work I go into, I know I want to be able to help people. I already have a job lined up and I'm pretty excited about it." She cleared her throat and looked like she was choosing her next words with deliberate care. "The new job comes with a lot of big life changes. I think I'm up to the challenge, though."

It was on the tip of my tongue to ask what kind of changes and challenges she was talking about when she suddenly flipped the conversation around to focus on me. She set her wine down on the table and leaned closer, eyes intense as she asked, "What about you? Had enough of war and being away from home? Or are you planning on being a career soldier?"

I lifted a shoulder and let it fall. "I'm good at what I do. I've advanced quickly since joining the army. As of now,

I have no plans to leave the military." I honestly wasn't sure what else was out there for me. I'd only graduated high school because my abuela threatened to kick me out of the house and cut off all contact with Gael if I didn't get my shit together. I'd done a lot of odd jobs and manual labor when I needed cash, but the army was where I'd finally figured out my value and the fact that I was a good leader, and had a knack for problem-solving in difficult situations.

Langley nodded and I watched with hungry eyes as her teeth suddenly dug into her full, lower lip. Her expression was still stoic and not giving much away, but I knew when she chewed on her lip like that, she was trying to hold words back.

"Isn't it hard to keep doing something where you never know if you're going to leave your loved ones behind for good? Doesn't it hurt every time you lose someone close to you for reasons out of your control? Since the first night we met, you told me everything you do is so your brother can have a better life, but what about you? What's your better life look like? When do you get a life that doesn't hurt all the time?"

I blinked in surprise at the question and leaned back in my chair. The tuxedo-clad waiter silently slipped up to the table and cleared the dessert plates. Langley had barely touched hers, and I could see one of her hands was tucked into a fist so tight her knuckles were turning white.

"I told you I grew up in a small town on the border in Texas, right?"

Langley nodded, strands of glimmering blonde hair sliding over her bare shoulders. My fingers itched to reach out and push it back behind her ear, but the girl had been flashing warning lights all night. She was here, but she was no longer mine to do with as I pleased. I couldn't touch without a clear invite.

"It wasn't a good environment, and there weren't a lot of options unless you wanted to sell drugs, or get your hands dirty. If I'd stayed in Texas, the people around me would still be dying, or they'd end up in jail. Losing a friend to gang violence or because they were tied up in drugs was an everyday occurrence. I probably wouldn't have had any other choice than to get myself tangled up in some bad stuff. Joining the army was a way out, and it was the only way I could bring in a steady income for my family. Being a soldier isn't easy—some days it feels like the worst job in the world—but this really is the version of my better life. It's dangerous, but it's always interesting, and I know whenever I lose someone I care about, or even someone I don't know, that they died for a cause that has meaning. They died because they made a choice to sacrifice for the greater good. I take the good with the bad, and I made my peace with my choice to be a soldier a long time ago."

"But isn't it frustrating for you not to know when you're going to leave next? How can you plan for a future when you have so little say over your own life?" Finally, some genuine emotion slipped through her icy veneer.

I reached out and put my hand over her clenched fist on the table. "I was focused on my brother's future, not my own, so it never made a difference. Meeting you changed all of that. I wasn't prepared to suddenly become a guy who wanted more." I rubbed my thumb across the back of her hand and waited until she looked up to meet my gaze.

"You made me want everything, and I didn't have the first clue how to ask for any of it. So, I left, because that's what I know how to do. I thought it would be easier on both of us, but I've never had anyone to miss before, no one who took up every single thought and feeling. I had no clue how hard it was going to be, or how much it was going to hurt. I hate myself for putting you through that."

She tugged her hand free and lowered it so that it disappeared beneath the table. The server, who really was dressed better than I was, dropped the bill. I saw Langley look at it and could practically feel her formulating an argument to hand it over. I slapped my credit card down before she could say anything, and frowned at her.

"You hated every single minute of this date, didn't you?" I wanted it to be special; instead, it was something she seemed to suffer through.

Langley shrugged and tilted her head to the side. "I don't hate it. It's just...not what I was expecting."

I frowned. "What do you mean?"

She sighed and lifted a hand to push her hair back behind her ear. "Last time you took me on a date, we played laser tag. It was fun. No one had ever taken me to do something like that before. This..." She waved a hand around the swanky restaurant. "I've been on twenty dates just like this one. The only thing special and unique about it is you."

I sucked in a sharp breath and fought the urge to slam my forehead down on the table. I wanted something memorable, and completely disregarded the fact that expensive and opulent were commonplace for her.

A tiny scowl pulled at her elegantly arched eyebrows. "Plus, I told you to stop spending money on me. I meant it."

This was the opposite of what I intended for the evening. I was trying to show her I could keep up with her lifestyle, but in doing so, I ran right over everything I already knew about her. She didn't need flashy and over the top. She needed something real, and tangible. Something solid.

Shaking my head at my own foolishness, I pocketed my credit card and climbed to my feet so I could pull her chair back and help her out of her seat. It was a quiet walk to my truck, each of us lost in thought. Out of the corner of my eye, I noticed Langley shiver. It wasn't exactly balmy in Colorado in May, and it rained earlier that day, so there was a bite in the air. Without a word, I slipped off my blazer—one she'd bought for me—and placed it over her shoulders. Her lacy top and flowy skirt didn't look like they would offer very much protection against the night chill.

Once we were in the truck, Langley did her best to smooth things over. She was always going to be a peacekeeper. The role was embedded in her DNA.

"Do you have any idea when you might have to deploy again? Do you even get the choice to stay in Colorado now that you're back?"

"I should be home for a while, and no, I don't know how long I may or may not be stationed here." There were always huge, looming uncertainties in my life. I didn't want her caught up in the cycle of wondering and worrying about whatever was next that I constantly lived in. "I've learned to be very adaptable over all these years of service."

"Going someplace new, learning a new job, meeting new people... it's exciting and scary at the same time, isn't it?" There was a note in her voice I couldn't place. I felt like she was saying more than her words indicated, but not for the first time tonight. I couldn't read her clearly.

"It is exciting and scary. I go into every transfer with the plan to make the most of it, to get the best experience I can from each new location. Wherever it is I'm going doesn't matter, what I do while I'm there does."

Out of the corner of my eye, I watched as she reached up to tug on her lower lip. The poor thing was getting abused tonight and all I wanted to do was kiss it and make it better.

"That's such a good way to look at things. I always found your perspective fascinating."

And I always found hers enlightening and enriching. We never failed to learn something from one another.

The drive to her apartment was short, and I could feel the tension between the two of us ratcheting up every minute that passed. She probably figured I was going to ask to come up to her place so we could pick up where we left off. I would bet good money she was trying to formulate a polite way to turn me down. Sure, if the date had gone better, I would be doing my best to end the night with her naked and underneath me in her bed. Considering how far off base I'd been, I knew she was nowhere near ready to let me back into her bed or her heart. There was still more work to do to prove I could do this, could be the kind of guy she wanted to keep around long-term. I wanted to be the guy worth waiting for.

When I pulled into a parking spot in front of her building, I felt, rather than saw, the way Langley tensed up. Letting out a bitter laugh, I dragged my hands down my face and muttered, "I don't suppose you'd give me a do-over. I know I said one date would be enough, but I feel like I really screwed this one up. I seem to do that a lot when it comes to you."

Langley sighed heavily and caused me to jolt when her very soft hand suddenly landed on my cheek. She used gentle pressure to turn my head in her direction and finally...*finally*...I could see everything she was feeling in those ocean-colored eyes.

Fear.

Pain.

Regret.

Joy.

Excitement.

Passion.

There were so many emotions, it was no wonder it'd been hard to pick one out from the rest.

"I like spending time with you, Iker. It doesn't matter what we do together, I always have a good time. I'm sorry if it didn't seem that way tonight, I was just processing some things. I have a lot on my mind lately, and everything is kind of jumbled up inside my head." She gave me a lopsided grin. "If I say yes to another date, you have to agree to let me plan it."

"Langley, if you agree to another date, I'll do anything you want me to."

I finally got a real smile from her, bright and almost blinding. She used her fingers to pinch my cheek, drawing a playful growl from my chest. "Walk me to my door and give me a goodnight kiss. That was my favorite part of our last date. But it ends with a kiss, though." She tapped her temple. "Anything more will make everything going on up here even more confusing. I still need some time to figure out how I really feel about you suddenly coming back into my life."

Stopping at a kiss might be one of the hardest things I'd ever been challenged with, but I could do it.

I hopped out of the truck and walked around the front so I could open the door for Langley. I offered her an arm to help her down, and was secretly pleased she left her fingers curled in the crook of my elbow as we walked to her door.

Once we reached it, Langley turned to look at me, and I leaned toward her, backing her against the door the same way I had the night I was drunk. Only, tonight she watched me lean closer with anticipation instead of fear. Her fingers trembled as she reached up and caught the knot of my tie. In a few quick moves, she had the expensive material hanging loose around my neck as her palms slid across my chest.

"I like you better without it." Her eyebrows winged up as she popped a couple of buttons open on my shirt. "I like it when it looks like you just rolled out of bed and threw whatever was closest on, because you still look better than most men wearing a thousand-dollar suit, and you look comfortable."

I brushed my knuckles across her cheekbone and lowered my head until our foreheads touched. She exhaled, and I swore I could taste the wine she had with dinner and her own, sweet flavor I could still clearly recall from the last time I kissed her.

"I like you in anything...anytime...anywhere." It was true. She was always the prettiest girl in the room to me, regardless of how she was dressed. My eyes followed her helplessly, and so did my heart.

I put my mouth on hers before she changed her mind.

Before she decided it was a bad idea.

Before she could remember how badly I'd hurt her the last time she let me get this close.

Her lips were warm and responsive under mine. She gave a breathy little sigh and allowed my searching tongue entrance into the damp, silky recesses of her mouth. Her tongue was quick and eager as it flicked against mine. Her hands were hot where they curled into the material of my shirt, pulling me closer as one of my hands tunneled into the long strands of hair at the back of her head, while the other rested at the base of her spine.

She made a soft, whimpering sound when my teeth nipped at the curve of her lower lip, and her hips pressed into mine as she lifted on the toes of her heels so she could get even closer. The kiss went from something sweet and seductive, to something explosive and sexy in the span of seconds. It didn't take long for all the kisses we'd missed, all the touches that had passed us by, all the time we'd lost to catch up to both of us.

Between one breath and the next, we went from saying goodbye to trying to devour one another.

One of Langley's hands latched onto my jaw, fingers digging in as she held me in place so her lips could voraciously move over mine. Her knee slid between my legs, and a moment later, I forgot my own name and where we were when I felt the press of her thigh against the raging hard-on trapped behind the zipper of my slacks. Her tongue swirled around mine, and it was my turn to make a noise when I felt the bite of her teeth against my lips.

I tilted my head to get a better angle and tugged her even closer. We were pressed chest to chest, hip to hip, and I could feel all of her most sensitive and malleable parts pressed against everything about me that was rigid and unyielding. My dick was ready to burst free of its confines, and I was having a hard time reminding it that this kiss was as far as things were going tonight. Why did I agree to that? Was I really going to be able to stop with just a kiss?

I had to. I was rebuilding her trust, and I wasn't going to fail the first test.

I felt Langley's thumb trace the flexing line of my jaw and bit back a moan when the tip of her tongue flicked across mine. The hand she had resting on my chest moved until her fingertips were touching the bare skin she'd exposed when she unbuttoned the front. The contented sigh she released feathered across my lips and made my cock throb hard enough it was almost painful.

She traced the pattern of one of the tattoos I had inked on my collarbone and slowly tilted her head back so she could look me in the eye.

"I missed this... Touching you...kissing you." She gave a delicate little snort. "I just missed you, Iker."

"I missed you, too, Langley." I shifted so I could kiss the top of her head and pulled her in tight for a hug that was more about comfort than sex. "So much."

Her hand rested over the spot on my chest where my heart was pounding, and I immediately fell backward when she applied a little pressure.

"I really want to invite you in, but I'm not going to." Her voice was so quiet I almost missed what she was saying.

"I get it. Last time we were together, it was a race. We have time, there's no need to rush things. Let's be careful and move slowly so we can get it right." I smoothed a hand over her silky hair and gave her a quick kiss before putting some breathing room between the two of us.

Langley shifted on her spiked heels and I narrowed my eyes as she audibly gulped. "Yeah. All the time in the world." She looked pale as she slipped my jacket off her shoulders and turned to shove the key in her door. "Thank you for tonight. Next date is my treat. I'll call you when I have something figured out."

I opened my mouth to respond, but she already slipped inside her apartment and I could hear the locks clicking shut.

Part of me was ecstatic she was committing to another date. A bigger, louder, scarier part of me was obsessing over why Langley looked like she was going to cry when I mentioned we could take things slow this time around.

I had a sinking feeling there was something she wasn't telling me and in a startling moment of clarity realized exactly how shitty it felt to be on the other side of caring for someone when they had a secret they weren't willing to share.

Karma was indeed a bitch, and it sucked that I deserved every bit of her current wrath.

Chapter 8

Langley

"Hey," I said to Sam as I peeked my head into his office.

He leaned back in his chair and smiled. "Hey, yourself."

"Thanks for letting me drop by." This was going to be awkward enough without me being a bitch over text message.

"No problem. The other guys are out and I have"—he glanced at the clock—"about half an hour before I have to head over to my next job. Come on in." He motioned to the armchair that flanked his desk, and I skirted around the other three desks in the room before taking the seat.

It wasn't fair to keep him on the hook. I knew I'd never put out a signal that said we'd get hot and heavy and exclusive, but there had been enough hope in his eyes that I had to be honest with him—with myself.

"I'm sorry for not calling." I nervously tucked a strand of hair behind my ear.

"I'd rather see you anyway. What's going on?" He turned his chair to face me, and I almost lost my nerve.

Sam really was a great guy. Gorgeous, fit, kind, smart, and hard-working. He just wasn't *my* great guy. Even if I was staying in Colorado—which I wasn't—this would have ended eventually. Kissing Iker last night showed me I'd never be satisfied without that intense level of hunger and need for my partner.

"So, I need to talk to you." I shifted my hands on my purse and pulled it into my lap, full of nervous energy. "And I don't think you're going to be happy with what I have to say."

His eyes lost that sparkle that had drawn me to him in the first place. "You're going back to him, aren't you? The guy from graduation?"

My eyes widened. "How did you know that was him?"

"Because I listen when you talk. I put two and two together that he was the guy who'd walked out on you after your sister's wedding." He looked up at the ceiling, obviously working his way through some intense feelings.

"I'm not really sure what's going on with me and Iker," I answered honestly. "It's not like we're back together, but I did go out with him last night." Honesty had been my policy with Sam since day one. I simply didn't have the energy or the need to play games. And, he was too nice of a guy for me to string along.

He looked at me with a small smile. "You know we're not exclusive. You can go on dates. Going out with him once doesn't mean you have to break up with me, if that's where this is headed."

Now I was smiling. "Can it really be called a breakup when we're not together?"

"Good point." He sighed and shook his head. "Do what you have to, but I think it's a bad idea. That guy busted you up pretty good the last time you trusted him."

"I know." I did. But my heart had proven to be pretty stupid when it came to Iker. "But it's not just Iker, Sam. I'm moving to Texas for my new job at the end of the month. You're actually the first person I'm telling outside of my family." I'd been so caught up in the whirlwind of emotions that always seemed to take over my life when Iker was part of it, to fill my family in on my major life changes.

His shoulders dipped in defeat. "Guess this really is a goodbye then."

"It is." There would be so many goodbyes in my future. What the hell was I thinking, restarting something with Iker when I couldn't finish it?

"Man, I'm sorry to hear that. Not that I'm not happy for you." He ran his hand over his beard. "You sure there's nothing I can say to change your mind? About the guy, not the job."

"The guy is..." I looked away, trying to come up with a not-so-dramatic way to describe Iker. Air? Electricity? A roller coaster with all the climbs, dips, and turns that made me feel alive? A total and complete risk?

"So, it's like that?" he said softly.

I looked back at him, only to see sadness etched in the lines of his mouth, but there was acceptance there too.

"Yeah, I guess it is."

"He's going to hurt you," he warned as I stood up. "You know it."

"Maybe," I admitted. "You're a fantastic guy, Sam. Really. And I know you'll find an equally fantastic woman."

He stood, shaking his head as he looked down at me. "You always were the long shot I couldn't help but take. I was never good enough for you, anyway."

I hugged him tight. "The opposite is true." He'd been nothing but good to the girl with a missing heart, because I'd never gotten it back from the thief who'd stolen it. "I was never good enough for you. Believe me."

"Well, if they can't come down on the price, then you tell them we're going to have to walk away. I have no problem structuring a buyout that protects their employees, but I'm sure as hell not going to line the pockets of those pension-stealing assholes in the front office."

I pushed through the mahogany door of my dad's home office and stood quietly, so I didn't disturb his phone call as he paced in front of his mahogany desk that matched the walls of mahogany bookshelves.

His smile was instant when he saw me, and he motioned me in. Out of habit, I kicked off my ballet shoes and sank into one of the brocade loveseats that made up the conversation set, curling my feet under my skirt.

"My line is drawn, Charles. Period. Handle it. My daughter needs me." He hung up without a farewell and tossed his phone onto the desk, then pressed a button.

"Yes, sir?"

"Barbara, could you please make up two cups of hot chocolate and bring them to my office? Extra marshmallows."

"Absolutely, sir."

I rolled my eyes as he took the loveseat across from mine. "You know it's May, right, Dad? Hot chocolate is more of a snowy day thing."

"Is it? I thought it was a Langley-has-something-on-her-mind thing." He shrugged out of his suit coat and draped it over the back of the couch.

"Okay, fine, you're right."

"Yes, I know." He settled in and leaned his elbow on the armrest. "Spill it."

So, I did. I told him about the effects of Iker showing up at graduation, and moved on to now being conflicted about the job offer and starting over in a completely different state. My father's shock was palpable. And so was his quiet amusement when I launched into a tirade about the crazy-expensive gifts, my trip to Iker's apartment, and the outright disaster that had been our date. I left out the kiss, because, well, no dad wanted to hear about his daughter's sex life, or lack thereof. I finished with everything that had gone down with Sam an hour ago.

As I finished up, Barbara knocked on the door, and Dad rose to help her open the door.

"You don't have to do that," she chided in the stern way a housekeeper with a decade under her belt had.

"I wanted to," Dad said, like always.

"Miss Langley! I didn't realize it was you! I should have, since it's not like this guy asks for hot chocolate in May." She handed me a steaming cup of hot, chocolatey goodness, topped with a mountain of marshmallows.

"Thank you, Barbara. I just popped in to talk to Dad for a second." I couldn't help but smile at the way she ordered my father to sit before handing him his own cup.

"Corbin, I need you—" Virginia waltzed through the door in this season's latest Chanel linen. "Oh, Langley, dear. I didn't know you were home." She forced a smile, which was almost polite for her.

"Just stopped in to see Dad for a minute," I repeated.

"Oh, no problem. This can wait. You two have—"

"Mom!" Camille's voice shattered the peace. "It's not right! The whole thing is blush and I asked for nude!"

"Virginia," Dad warned.

She sighed. "I'll handle her. Pregnancy hormones and all. Langley." She pretty much swept out of the office. As interactions went, this was mellow...almost cordial.

I had a sneaking suspicion Dad had finally intervened on my behalf with his wife. The claws were now mostly sheathed and the snide remarks uttered under her breath instead of barked in my face.

"Cami and Richard are supposed to be getting their own house in two months," Dad said slowly, like it was a mantra.

"Two months too long," Barbara muttered as she left.

Dad gave me a long, probing look and returned the conversation to my suddenly unpredictable and unsteady. "Have you told me everything?"

I took a sip of my chocolate and nodded.

"And do you need an ear or advice?" he asked, then sipped on his own.

"Advice." I loved that about him. His willingness to provide either at my discretion.

"Well, first, I'm incredibly proud of you for landing that job. Overland is a pain in my ass, but that's a top-notch firm he runs. As much as I would have killed to have you at Vaughn, I respect your need to make it on your own. Doesn't mean I'll give up hope that you'll eventually return to take over the family empire, of course." He saluted me with his mug.

"Yeah, yeah. I love you, and Vaughn, but I'm not spending my early years being known as the boss's daughter. No, thank you."

"I'll miss you," he said quietly, his expression falling. "I figured you'd go away to school, and when you chose Colorado College, I was overjoyed. Not that I didn't know this was coming, but still...I'll miss you."

"I'll miss you too," I admitted.

"But enough about my feelings. Let's talk about yours. What are you going to do about Iker?"

"I have no clue." I sipped my chocolate down, wishing the answer would appear in the bottom of the cup. "That date wasn't him. Wasn't us. Any of the guys I've dated would have done the same thing, and I know he can't afford it either. I just wanted to go out with *him*. It's like he's trying to shove himself into the mold of what he thinks I want."

"That's exactly what he's doing." Dad set his mug on the table between us and leaned on his knees. "Look, I have mixed feelings about that young man. That's no secret. I hate what he did to you, but I love the effect he had on you. For the first time in your life, there was a color in your face that wasn't cosmetic. You looked...alive. You started to raise your voice, to really advocate for yourself, and I can't ignore that Iker was the root of you finding your backbone. Hell, I'm thankful for it. So, if you're asking me if I think you should give him a shot, then..."

He sighed and glanced over my shoulder, where I knew he kept a framed picture of my mother. It was the only one Virginia hadn't banned.

"Then I think you should follow your heart, because the people who can really change us for the better are few and far between."

"He hates our world. He hates the fake people and the entitlement, and the obscene waste of money. He hates everything about how we live." I took in what had to be almost a million dollars in first edition books behind a glass case. "But, he's trying to pretend he doesn't so we have some common ground." I was changing him for the worse.

"Yeah, well, I do too." Dad shrugged. "Okay, I love the money. I like nice things and I love giving you opportunities other kids don't get. But the rest of it? That's just the society, sweetheart, not the world. He knows you're nothing like Camille, or any of the others in that circle."

He looked at me with such love, such openness, and it turned the guilt over in my stomach like nothing else could. "You don't know everything about him. About us."

"Oh, you mean that you paid him ten thousand dollars to be your date to Cammy's wedding?" His eyebrows twitched.

I fumbled, nearly losing my chocolate all over the brocade sofa we were sitting on, then put it next to his on the table. "You knew?"

"I assumed. Your accountant called and told me you'd pulled ten thousand dollars from your trust fund the week before, and then Iker showed up, this guy you'd never once mentioned, but all of a sudden had a relationship with. I'm not a genius, sweetheart, but I can do math, and one plus one equals two." There was zero judgment or condemnation in his eyes.

"You knew. My accountant what?" I sputtered.

"I have financial oversight on your trust fund until you're twenty-five. Your mom didn't want you to blow it all in Vegas or something." He shrugged.

"You knew and didn't say anything that whole week?"

"Watching you two was a hell of a lot more entertaining than anything to do with the wedding, especially when you guys developed feelings for each other. That was pretty obvious too."

"I'm...speechless."

He grinned. "Nice to know I can still pull one over on you. Look, if you want to give it a go with him, then just make sure he understands two things. The first is that you want him, and not who he thinks you should want. And second, I'll fucking kill him if he hurts you again."

I pressed my lips in a straight line to keep from laughing. "And when I move?"

He looked over at my mom again. "If he's fun, then you have fun. There's no harm in that. If he's the one, then you tackle it like you do everything else—head-on and honest."

As I got ready to leave, he hugged me tight. "You know, I saw that you paid the college tuition of two students with your fund too."

I tensed, waiting for the lecture.

"That's something your mother would have done. I'm proud of your heart, Langley, and I know your mom is too."

I couldn't help but wonder if that same heart was about to get me into a heap of heartbreak again.

"I didn't realize you could check out dogs like library books." Iker laughed, throwing the tennis ball again. Einstein chased it across the open space of the state park, his fluffy fur bouncing with each bound.

"It's a perk of volunteering there." I held my hand over my eyes to watch Einstein race back to us with a slobbery yellow ball in his mouth. "And I kind of have it bad for this guy. You didn't have to come, you know. Our date doesn't technically start for another two hours." Not that I was arguing against more Iker time, but this wasn't the date I'd planned.

"I told you I was up for anything, and besides, I have short work days since we just got back."

"I'm glad you came." Maybe it was because there was no pressure of being on a planned date, but this felt easy. More like what we used to be like.

"Me too. You know, you could always adopt him," he suggested as he wrestled the ball from Einstein's mouth. "Hey, you have to give it back if you want me to throw it again."

Einstein let it go.

"No pets are allowed in my building." Of course, I'd asked. And I had no clue what awaited me in Texas. I'd already started searching for apartments and townhouses, but it was hard to decide without actually seeing anything, and I was having a little bit of sticker shock. Austin was way more expensive than Colorado Springs, especially if I wanted to live downtown.

Iker threw the ball again, and I watched the play of muscles in his arm with far more interest than I should have. "That's a tough rule. I hate that I'm not dependable enough for a dog. I'm away for weeks at a time for training, and when deployment hits, what would I do? I'd never be the asshole dropping him at the pound, and I don't exactly know a lot of people who aren't on the same fucked-up schedule I am."

"That sounds lonely."

"It can be. But it's just as lonely for the ones we leave behind." He looked at me meaningfully.

I ripped my gaze away as Einstein flew back at us. "Okay, one more, and then you're due back at the jail," I warned him, crouching to get the ball. "You ready?" I stood and threw the ball, then laughed as Einstein flopped his way toward it.

"I like you like this," Iker said softly.

"Like what?" I made the mistake of looking up at him and was instantly sucked into his eyes, the curve of his lower lip, and his damned dimple that peeked out as he grinned.

"No expectations or rules to follow." His finger trailed over the bare skin of my shoulder where it met my tank top strap. "You're hot as hell in dresses and heels, trust me, but there's something about seeing you unpolished that does it for me."

Everything about him did it for me. Pretty sure my temperature spiked the minute he'd pulled up in his truck.

"You only had one normal date with me last summer. Everything else was wedding-oriented. Did you ever stop to think that maybe I'm closer to average than what you saw? You only got a glimpse of my life, Iker. Just a little slice, not the whole cake."

Einstein raced back to us, and I stole the ball away.

"There's nothing about you that's average," Iker said as we walked back to his truck. "But I'm starting to see the bigger picture, and I like everything I see. Now, what are we up to next?"

"Well, we're dropping Einstein at doggy jail, then I need to run home and change really quick, if that's okay." I scrunched my nose. "I didn't think about that when we started early."

"Do I need to change?" He motioned to his simple t-shirt and jeans.

"No, you look perfect for what I have in mind." I let my eyes sweep down his frame and almost groaned at the wave of pure want that washed over me. It didn't help matters that I knew he looked even better under those clothes. That I knew the taste of his skin and the many wicked ways he used his mouth and tongue on my skin too.

"And what might that be?" His eyes flared with hunger.

"Kicking your ass."

"You weren't kidding." Iker shook his head as I chalked up my pool cue. The jukebox blared eighties' hair metal and I shrugged with a grin. I'd just run the table on him while he gawked, and damn, did it feel good.

"Hey, I told you not to hold back. Losers rack." I nodded toward the wooden rack that hung on the dingy wall.

"That's the last time I take it easy on you," he answered with a grin. "Where the hell did you learn to play pool?"

"At home." I slipped quarters into the slots and pushed the lever in, releasing the balls in a rush. I took them out one by one, rolling them to Iker, who racked them for our next game of eight-ball. "Yeah, yeah, I know, little rich girl with a pool table. But it was a fun way for me and Dad to spend time together, and I learned a ton about business when his clients came over to play."

"Business at the pool tables, huh? I did a little of that myself. Of course, it had more to do with betting, and less to do with hedge funds." He shrugged.

"Look who's been reading up on financials." My eyebrows rose, and he laughed as I sent the last ball his way.

"Figured if it had you interested, then it had to be something worth a Google search or two." He looked around the pool hall, which was only half full since it was a weeknight. "How did you find this place?"

"Do you mean, how on Earth did I step outside my Broadmoor bubble to discover the miracle of pool halls? Or this place, in particular?" I backed up into the barstools and took my beer off the small table.

"Both," he answered, shoving his fingers into the back of the rack to tighten the formation before removing the wooden frame.

"Last year, one of my girlfriends tracked her boyfriend down here after getting the hey-he's-too-drunk-to-drive phone call from his buddy. I went with her, and when he wouldn't leave, I made him agree that if I beat him in a game, he'd come with us."

"And I'm guessing he left quietly?"

"I almost lost that game," I answered truthfully, lining up the cue ball to break. "I didn't realize that the table I'd been playing on was way bigger than these babies. Threw me off. But yeah, he left. He was pretty pissed about getting beat by a girl too."

I leaned down, putting myself eye level with the ball, and stroked the cue once to line up my shot. "I told him not to worry since I play like a boy." I pulled back and shot, breaking the balls apart. They flew to the ends of the table, two falling in. "Stripes," I called.

"You play like a boy?" Iker questioned, watching me move around the table. "Because you sure as hell look all woman to me."

I hadn't missed the way his eyes darkened when I walked out of my room wearing a pair of skin-tight jeans and blue halter top. The same way they were locked on my ass right now. I chose the ball right across from where he stood. "Twelve in the side."

He cocked his head to the side, but didn't question my choice.

"You see, the girls in the sorority played like this," I leaned over moderately, keeping my head far above the table and arching my back to put my breasts on display.

"Uh. Huh." His eyes went straight to my assets and he shifted his weight.

"But one, I'd been taught by my dad, and two"—I flattened my back and took my position—"I wasn't out here to attract guys since I wasn't over you." My eyes locked with his for a second, and then I sank the shot. "Guys weren't on my agenda."

"The whole time I was gone, you didn't..." Iker let the question hang.

"Did you?" I countered, choosing another position. "Fourteen, corner pocket. And don't tell me that you didn't have the opportunity. I'm well aware that there were plenty of women with you on that deployment." I knew how to do a Google search as well.

The shot was tricky with the ball kissed up against the two. I leaned down and lined her up.

"I didn't," Iker answered, coming up behind me. "And you're right, there were women, and yeah, it's not exactly allowed, but things like that happen over there."

Chills shot down my spine as he ran a fingertip from the tie at the base of my neck to where my shirt began just above the back clasp of my bra. "Oh? Why not?"

I slid the cue through my hand, practicing the shot.

"None of them were blonde enough," he whispered as his lips grazed the top of my ear. "Their eyes weren't blue enough, their smiles were never bright enough. None of them had legs that invaded my dreams, or skin so damn touchable that I couldn't think."

My heart pounded against my ribs, and my breath hitched, but I took the shot.

And missed.

"I wasn't interested in any of them," he continued as I slowly stood. "Because I only wanted you."

I turned, our bodies meeting with maddening friction as I brought my eyes up to meet his. God, that smolder was going to be the death of me. He wasn't just sexy, he was sex incarnate, advertised in the build of his body, the tattoos that may as well have been warning signs, and the promise in his eyes.

"That last night with you..." He splayed one hand on my lower back and pressed us even closer. "It ruined me. You're like a drug. The first hit pulled me in and left me with the kind of craving that keeps an addict up at night."

I swallowed as the tips of my breasts hardened against his chest. "You can't say things like that. Not when we said we're taking this slow."

The corner of his mouth lifted. "I didn't say everything I wanted to the last time. I'm not making the same mistake twice. And if it makes you feel uncomfortable, then that's just too damn bad."

I shifted my hips against his dick and he sucked in a breath. "I'm not the one who feels *uncomfortable*." He really hadn't touched another girl in the time we'd been apart? It was hard to imagine anyone with Iker's sex drive not, well...*driving*. "I kissed Sam once, but you already knew that." He tensed, and I cupped his neck with my empty hand. "But that was it. The last man to touch me—really touch me—was you."

Something hot and possessive flashed in his eyes.

"And I told Sam yesterday that I wasn't going to see him anymore." I whispered the confession.

"You did?"

"Yep." Shit, there was that dimple again. I swore he knew how much I loved that damn thing and used it against me on purpose. "Now move. It's your shot."

"Yeah, it is," he agreed, stepping backward. "Let's make it interesting. What will you give me if I win?"

I cocked an eyebrow at him. "What do you want?"

"A kiss," he answered. "Just a kiss."

"What do I get?"

"Anything you want that I can give." He lined up his shot, and my eyes were drawn to his ass like a magnet.

I had no idea what I would ask for. A kiss? More? For him to fabricate more time so I could spend it with him? A promise to visit me when I left? The thought sliced into my heart with surgical precision.

"We on?" he asked, looking up at me from where he leaned over the table.

"We're on," I promised.

He ran the fucking table.

"Are you kidding me?" I asked as he walked me out of the pool hall fifteen minutes later. The parking lot was poorly lit, but I never worried about my safety when I was with Iker. He'd wiped that concern from my mind the first time we'd met.

"What?" He looked down at me with mock innocence, but took my hand.

"You let me win the first game?" I accused. "You're a hustler."

"No. I wouldn't do that. The first one, you ran the table off the first shot, and I didn't even get to play. The second and third, I was having too much fun watching your ass to care if I sank a shot. You're fucking formidable. And one hell of a distraction."

"And the fourth?" I questioned as we reached his truck.

"I had a very good reason to win."

Instead of opening the door and climbing into the truck, I put my back against the cool metal and looked up at him. "How did you learn to play like that?" I gave him his own question.

"Unlike you, I *did* learn on tables that size. And I wasn't kidding. I did earn some money betting. I just didn't mention that I put the money on myself." He put his palms on either side of my head, caging me in. Total hustler, but it was much better than him trying to conform and confine himself to five-star standards.

"There's so much I don't know about you." I knew his character, his kindness, and even his sharp edges, but not the details, the history, or the little pieces of him that made the whole.

"We have time," he promised in that sandpaper-rough voice.

But we didn't. Not enough.

"Do I get to claim my prize?" he asked.

"Here?" I glanced around the quiet parking lot, not really caring where he kissed me as long as he did.

"Trust me, it's safer than your apartment." His eyebrows lifted.

"Claim away." Getting to kiss him, and being kissed by him, made us both winners in my book.

His mouth met mine in blatant hunger. His kiss was demanding, and I opened for him out of pure instinct, letting a moan loose when our tongues met and tangled.

There was nothing on Earth that compared to kissing Iker. His hands tangled through the hair at the nape of my neck, pins flying from where I'd pinned up the strays from my ponytail. I rose on my toes, cursing the sensible choice of wearing Vans, and wishing I'd had the height advantage of heels. The need to get closer drove my hands to wind around his neck as his drifted to my hip.

He angled my head to kiss me deeper and I answered with a whimper, flicking my tongue with his until he groaned and sank into the kiss, pressing me back against the truck. It wasn't enough. It was never enough with him.

As if he read my mind, his grip shifted to my ass, and he used both hands to lift me to eye level, never breaking the kiss. My legs wrapped around his warm waist as my back absorbed the heat from the cool metal of the truck.

"Langley," he rasped against my lips.

My thighs locked as my whole core turned molten, liquid. Then I had one hand in his hair and another clutching the muscles of his arm as I gently bit his lower lip, sucking it into my mouth.

His grip tightened on my ass and he changed the tempo of the kiss, using his tongue to remind me exactly what he could do with the magnificent body I was wrapped around. My nerves hummed and sizzled as I rocked into him, taking everything he offered in the kiss and demanding more.

I wanted it all.

He ripped his mouth away from mine. "We have to stop."

I chased his lips and took them again, swallowing his low rumble of half-hearted protest. Then my tongue rubbed against his and he sucked it into his mouth. My nails bit little half moons into his skin as he broke the kiss to press heated ones against my jaw, then my neck.

"Iker," I whimpered when he sucked at a sensitive spot.

His chest heaved as he moved, and I heard the door to the truck open. Yep, this was good. I'd take whatever I could have of him before I lost him forever...again.

My ass hit the cushion, when I moved to scoot back so he could slide over me, he tore his mouth from mine and used his hands to turn my legs so I was sitting. Then he shut the door and leaned back against it.

He was on the wrong damn side.

"Really?" I questioned, trying and failing to get my breathing under control. I was on fire for him, all common sense burnt up in his touch.

"Really?" he answered as the back of his head hit the window with a *thunk*. "We said slow, remember?"

"You said slow," I muttered, knowing damn well he'd done the right and honorable thing.

A minute later, he climbed into the driver's seat and only glanced my way to make sure my seatbelt was on before he drove us out of the parking lot. "God, I almost forgot what it was like to kiss you," he swore. "You steal every logical thought out of my head besides how fast I can get your clothes off."

I didn't tell him I was on board with that. Honestly, the logical part of me was cheering him on, knowing I'd regret it. But what if I didn't? What if he really was the one, and we were wasting time by holding back?

"Sorry," he muttered, throwing me a wry grin. "I had to stop us before we took it too far to come back from. We have time. We have time." He muttered that last part to himself like a vow.

"I get it," I answered, reassuring him with a nod. But the truth was, we had already gone too far to come back, and we *didn't* have time.

For the first time, I wondered if this was how he'd felt last summer, falling into each other while he knew it couldn't last.

Call this what it is. What it was. An eclipse. A comet. Whatever. Something raw and rare that only comes around once in a lifetime that changes you—and then leaves.

His words came to me so clearly, he might as well have said them from the driver's seat, rather than written them in the letter sitting in my glove box.

He'd been wrong, though. This rare thing had come around twice, but this time, it would be me who left.

For the first time since getting the job offer, I seriously thought about staying.

Chapter 9

Iker

"I'm going to ask you to come in with me tonight." Langley sounded breathless, and I could barely contain the urge to throw a fist up in victory at her words. However, in order to do that, I'd have to pull my hand out from underneath her shirt, and I wasn't about to do something that stupid. Not when the windows of my truck were fogged up and both of us had clothing out of place and askew from impatient hands seeking skin. We'd been spending a lot of time together the last week, and each goodnight kiss was steamier, and hotter, than the one before it. One of us always managed to put on the brakes before things got too carried away, but I was sick of jerking off while thinking of her, the same way I had while I was deployed.

I was by no means a saint, and my patience had been put to the test unlike it ever had before. I kept reminding myself she was worth whatever hoops I needed to jump through, we were worth the work.

"I want you to come inside with me, but I need to tell you something first." Langley wrapped her fingers around my wrist and firmly tugged at my hand until I pulled my hand free from her bra. The serious tone of her voice made my spine stiffen, and the worried look in her eyes had all the alarm bells I possessed ringing so loud I couldn't hear myself think.

I knew something was up with her.

Over the last few days, we dated like a normal couple. We went to the movies. I took her to lunch so she could spend some time with my brother, and I was thrilled how well they hit it off. I let her drag me to something called a garden party, and I wheeled and dealed, so I could get my hands on tickets to see *Wicked* in Denver. The seats were shitty, and I hated the crowded, dark theater, but Langley loved every minute of it, and her smile was worth any amount of discomfort I had to put myself through. We were learning everything about each other, and I could feel our bond getting tighter, but I knew she was keeping something from me.

There were a handful of times I caught her watching me with tears in her eyes. I lost count of all the times she opened her mouth to say something, only to snap it closed a moment later. When I asked her what was up, she flashed that fake smile I loathed when it made an appearance, and she would quickly change the subject. I didn't have much room to press her, considering the huge secret I'd kept from her the last time we were together. So, I was stuck waiting for her to decide if she trusted me enough to tell me what she'd obviously been struggling with.

I pulled away from her and practically threw myself against the driver's side door of my truck. I dragged a hand down my face and silently ordered my dick to behave. I tapped the knuckles of one hand against my temple and told Langley, "Shoot."

She twined her fingers together and I watched as she visibly tried to psych herself up to say whatever it was that was so important.

"I want you to stay the night with me. I want you to be there when I wake up this time." Her eyes were practically pleading with me, and I had to work really hard to keep the dread crawling up the back of my throat from showing on my face. "But, if you can't do either of those things after I tell you what's going on in my life right now, I understand and I won't hold any choice you make against you."

I frowned. "What the hell, Langley?" I was lost, and fear was starting to work its way under my skin.

"I'm moving to Austin at the end of the month." The words burst out in a rush and I could see the admission made her shake from head to toe. "I was offered a job... my dream job. I have to go. I accepted the offer before you came back into my life." She lifted a hand and put it on the base of her throat. I heard her gulp as she shifted nervously across from me. "Honestly, I would have accepted the job even if you were in my life. It's everything I ever wanted to do with my degree, and I'll be helping so many people. I don't know what it means for us as a couple, if we even are a couple, but I know we can't be in a situation where one of us knows what's coming and the other is clueless. Not again." She made a move like she was going to reach out and touch me, but pulled back at the last second. "I'm not sure where we go from here."

Langley sounded absolutely despondent and lost. Fitting, since her words made me feel the same way.

Laughing, mostly so I didn't cry, I tossed my head back and let it bang on the window behind me. "Our timing fucking sucks."

She exhaled loudly, the sound turning into something close to a sob. "It really does."

I groaned and closed my eyes. "Obviously, you know it's not up to me where and when I go somewhere new. I can request a transfer, but nothing is certain." I couldn't drop everything and follow her, even if I wanted to. Which, I wasn't sure I did. I had spent my entire childhood trying to get out of Texas. Did I really want to go back just because the girl I couldn't forget was going to be there?

"I know, and I'd never expect you to uproot your entire life for me. It almost seems like the universe is trying to keep us from being together." She blew out a breath, sending her hair dancing on her forehead. My gaze lingered on her kiss-swollen lips and the flush in her cheeks. She was too pretty for my peace of mind.

I swore and let the silence surround us so I could have a quick moment to process how I felt about this new dynamic.

At the end of the day, was her having to leave for a job she loved and wanted to excel at any different than me having to leave to do mine? The only difference was, I'd be the one waiting. I'd be the one sitting on pins and needles, worrying and wondering while we were apart. Sure, her job didn't involve war and warriors, but she said she was going to be helping people, and that was the same thing I did every time I deployed, be it people back home or abroad.

"We're destined to have distance between us." Not just physical distance, but even the enormous distance in our social status and economic backgrounds was huge. "One of us is always running after the other."

Langley made a soft sound, and a moment later, her hand landed on my forearm. Her fingers dug in and her voice shook as she told me, "I don't mind the chase as long as one of us eventually catches the other. If that's too much to ask, I get it. We've only known each other a short time. We're both still young. It would be so much easier for both of us if we decide to walk away. At least this time, the decision would be mutual." She blinked rapidly and I knew she was on the brink of bursting into tears. "I won't feel so powerless, so betrayed, this time."

I caught the first tear that fell with my index finger. Her skin was like velvet when I wiped it away. I promised myself I would stop being the reason she cried, but I should have known it wouldn't be that easy. Seeing her so upset and worried, and feeling the visceral reaction to her tears deep in my gut, I grabbed her hand in mine and pulled her across the seat into a tight hug.

"Let's go up to your apartment." A long-distance relationship was the last thing I wanted...any relationship, really. But, if that was my only option to keep this woman in my arms, then I'd make it work.

She wasn't asking for anything more than what I'd eventually have to ask of her.

Langley sniffed against the hollow of my throat, and I felt her hands curl into the material of my t-shirt. "Are you going to be next to me in the morning?"

Of course, she had to ask. Who could blame her?

"I will be. I'll always be there, from here on out. We *are* a couple. We will figure out a way to make this work."

I didn't know how, but I told her I would be the solution to our problems moving forward, and I meant it.

I blindly groped for the door handle, sending both of us tumbling out. I caught Langley before she hit the ground and pulled her behind me as I walked purposefully toward her apartment. I wasn't looking back. I wasn't going to question my decision to stick things out with her. Love hurt. I could feel the sting of it in every cell and pore of my body, but the pain didn't overshadow the soft, warm glow surrounding my heart.

Her hands were shaking so bad, I had to take the keys from her and open the door. She tripped over nothing when she followed me into the apartment, her expression slightly dazed and bewildered. It was clear she thought I was going to run. She believed I was going to take the out she so conveniently provided. I still had a long way to go to show her just how serious I was about her...about us.

Her apartment was swanky and far more elegantly decorated than mine. Everything matched and was obviously high-end. It was all very Langley, down to the family photos scattered about. There were several of her with her parents when she was younger. Many of just her and her dad, and lots of a woman whom I guessed was her mother. There was a picture of her sandwiched between her father and another man, both dressed in formal military regalia. I knew her old man served when he was my age, but I was taken aback when I recognized the other guy in the picture as the general in command of my current base.

Distracted, I wasn't ready for Langley to take charge of the situation, and went easily as she jerked me into her bedroom. The space was as fancy and feminine as the rest of the apartment. It also smelled flowery and sweet, a scent I associated with her. Her bed looked pillowy and soft. I couldn't wait to make a mess if it...and her.

Langley hit a switch, and low light filtered through the room. I turned to face her, so I could tell her everything would be okay, and was taken completely off guard when her palms suddenly hit the center of my chest as she used my surprise to push me backward onto the bed.

I let out a little grunt as her hands hurriedly slid under the hem of my shirt and worked the fabric up my torso and over my head. My abs tensed involuntarily when she climbed on top of me, knees on either side of my hips as her quick fingers went to work on my belt and the fastening of my jeans. We'd been here before, her hands on me, mine on her. But something about this felt different. Felt new and exciting. There wasn't anything between us this time. No secrets. No lies. No subterfuge and no looming shadows of money and desperation. This time, we were honest about how we felt and the challenges us deciding to be together were going to present going forward. We weren't afraid of the future, but we were both aware if we wanted one together, we were going to have to work for it.

"Lift." Her eyebrows winged up as she tugged on my belt loops.

I kicked off my Chucks and complied with her sexy command. A moment later, I was sprawled naked on the bed beneath her as her fingertips trailed over the different images inked on my skin. She bent forward, her lips landing on the center of my chest as one of her palms skimmed over my ribs. I shifted under her, body

111

responding visibly as the ends of her hair slid across my skin. Everywhere she touched felt like a small electric shock buzzed through me.

"I remembered you like this when you were gone. You're really pretty without your clothes on, Alvarez." The tip of her tongue flicked over one of my nipples and I almost came up off the bed.

I trapped her head between my hands, fingers tangling in her silky hair as her lips danced even lower. Her nose touched my stomach and muscles tensed and flexed. I felt her smile against my skin, and my cock throbbed and begged for attention where it was pressed against the round curve of her backside.

"Same goes, Vaughn." In fact, I would be thrilled if she started shedding clothing right now.

All coherent thought fled when she wiggled her way down my body, lips and tongue dragging the length of my abs, and lower. Everything contracted and went taut at the contact. I let out a moan when the tip of my now rigid and damp cock brushed the inside of Langley's thigh.

The top of my head felt like it was going to blow off, and I was ready to crawl out of my skin when her hand suddenly wrapped around the base of my dick and squeezed. I swore and used my hold on her head to bring her face upward so she had to meet my gaze. The mischievous glint in her blue eyes let me know she was firmly aware of the fact that she currently had all the power. I was putty in her hands. I couldn't stop her, not that any sane man would want to.

The first sweep of her tongue across the pulsing tip of my cock brought my shoulders off the mattress. The second swirl made my hands curl around her head and mutter her name on a broken sound. When the wet heat of her mouth surrounded the first few inches, I might've blacked out for a moment because it had been so long, and it felt so good. More than all of that, because it was Langley, it felt better than it had any right to. The entire act was more intimate, more meaningful than it had ever been in the past. She wasn't simply blowing my dick, but my mind, as well.

Both my brain and my heart were involved in every little move she made, every touch, every taste. Considering I typically only responded with what was between my legs when it came to sex, being with her was on an entirely different level. She took me to heights I'd never reached before, and there was no way I was ever going back to boring and basic.

She stroked her hand up the straining length that seemed to get harder and harder with each passing minute. She lowered her head at the same time, sucking in until her cheeks hollowed when they touched her fist. The dual stimulation felt so good, my hips lifted, blindly chasing the pressure and suction. Her tongue flicked against the leaking slit, causing my eyes to roll back in my head as my hands pulled at her hair, asking for more and begging for mercy.

It took every ounce of self-control I had not to explode in her mouth when her tongue danced along the thick vein running along the underneath side of the unyielding flesh in her mouth. She was alarmingly talented with that mouth of hers. Even if I hadn't already been willing to move mountains and slay dragons for her, I would be willing to do whatever she wanted after letting her take me apart with her lips and tongue.

"Jesus, Langley." I squeezed my eyes shut and tried to pull myself back from the brink. "I'm going to be done before we even get started."

She lifted her head and let go of my cock with a slick *pop*. It was sexy as hell, and the way she looked at that moment and the sounds would be seared in my mind forever.

"Just trying to bring you up to speed, soldier. I was ready to jump you the minute you said you'd be here when I woke up." She blinked at me, long lashes falling to cover her bright eyes. "I've been ready since the day you left. No one has ever made me feel the way you do, Iker. People tell me I'm pretty or beautiful all the time. Most of them want something. Most of them don't even see me. You're the only one who makes me feel beautiful. I like the way I look through your eyes."

"Jesus, woman." I'd lost my vocabulary along with my restraint.

Langley let out a yelp of surprise when I suddenly flipped us over. Once she was the one spread out on the designer bed set, I started peeling her out of her clothes. Once she was as naked as I was, I dropped to my knees by the side of the bed, tossed her toned and tanned legs over my shoulders, and put my mouth on her soft, sweet center. She was hot, and wet. She hadn't been kidding when she said my assurance I was sticking around this time really did it for her.

Her slick center quivered around my tongue and my name echoed off her bedroom walls. Immediately, her taste flooded my mouth and tingled across my tongue. The flavor was the same, and it made my dick twitch impatiently. When she started to whimper and squirm against my mouth, I pulled back after leaving a messy kiss on the inside of her smooth thigh. I needed to make sure she was as ready as she said she was, because there was no way I could handle her like she was fragile and breakable after being without her for so long. I flipped her around so she was on her hands and knees, facing away from me, and gruffly asked her to dig the lone condom out of my wallet. I grinned when she handed the foil packet over her shoulder without looking at me.

"I swear, the next time I'll go slow." Maybe. She made me crazy and forget myself.

Her hair slithered across her shoulders, and her back arched. Her eyes glinted like sapphires when she peeked at me over her shoulder.

"As long as there is a next time, I don't care if it's fast or slow. I want it...want you."

Well, fuck. I finally understood how a few words could turn her on and have her ready to go.

I put my hands on the sexy curve of her hips and pulled her to the edge of the bed. She gasped and her head fell forward. Her body rocked back against mine as I leaned forward so I could kiss my way up the long, elegant line of her spine. I took my cock in my hand and lined myself up with her velvety soft, and thoroughly soaked, opening.

Langley moved backward and met my first thrust. The room was instantly filled with quiet moans and the erotic sound of our bodies colliding. Her body clamped down on mine, the smooth, silken inner muscles squeezing and contracting around the solid length pushing deeper and throbbing in time to our heartbeats. Langley whispered my name and tossed her head back. My head dropped until my forehead rested between her shoulder blades. Her skin was slick with a light sheen of sweat, but she still smelled like a field of fresh flowers.

My hips moved of their own accord, rocking faster, pushing harder, chasing after the pleasure that was ratcheting up with each passing minute. I heard Langley moan, and the sound had me swearing against her soft skin.

I braced one hand on the bed beside her and snaked the other around to her front, fingers finding the pebbled point of her nipple. I rolled the velvety nub across my palm and traced across the goose bumps that lifted across her back with my tongue. She panted, her hips slipping out of rhythm as she mindlessly sought her own completion.

Desire exploded in bursts of white light behind my eyelids as pleasure coiled tightly at the base of my spine. I felt my stomach tighten and my breath quickened as her body went liquid and pliable around mine. She whispered my name, and possibly that she loved me, but I was too far gone and lost in my own spiraling satisfaction to let her words sink in. I used the hold I had on her chest to pull her up so her back was pressed against my front. There was no space between us, no lies, no dirty deals. It was just me and her, how I wished it had been from the start. I would never take for granted how damn lucky I was this woman with the world at her feet had picked me.

I buried my nose in her hair and let waves of absolute gratification pull me under. I could drown in a sea of bliss, but I had someone else to worry about, so I circled my hand around the base of Langley's throat and tilted her head to the side so I could kiss the outer shell of her ear, grinning as her entire body shivered along mine in response.

"You good?"

She nodded, one of her hands lifting to cover mine. "Never been better."

I snorted out a small laugh and kissed her cheek. "Give me a few and I'll prove you wrong." I could make her feel even better when I wasn't in such a rush to get inside of her.

She sighed in contentment and rubbed her head against me like a cat. "You're on." Her fingers curled around mine and her voice lowered. "I don't want to lose this again, Iker."

I tightened my arms around her, holding on like I would never let go. "Me either."

I never thought I would find this feeling, or someone I would want to wait for me... Someone I was willing to wait for.

I didn't know much about love, aside from the way I loved my family. But I knew with absolute certainty Langley was my first...love. My only love. She was the only one who made me believe I'd earned a shot at happiness. If there was anything worth fighting what seemed insurmountable odds to be together, it was that.

Chapter 10

Langley

I threw my carry-on into the trunk of my car and shut the hatch. Three days in Austin property hunting had been exhausting. Not that there weren't cute houses to choose from in Texas—all of which had air conditioning, that wasn't up for debate—but I'd been preoccupied with thoughts of Iker, and what it would be like to live in those houses without him.

Suddenly, those cute houses weren't quite so appealing.

Grumbling under my breath, I shot off a text to let the man constantly on my mind know I was back.

Langley: Just landed and headed home. Come over for dinner?

I slid behind the wheel of my car, swearing at the heat of the sun-scorched seats.

My phone buzzed with his reply before I could even get the car in gear.

Iker: I'll be over after work. Missed you.

A smile tugged at my lips. The clock read three, which meant I only had a few hours before I could see him.

Langley: Perfect. Come whenever you can. Missed you, too.

How often in the next—God only knew how long— would we say we missed each other in texts? Was it possible to keep a relationship alive that way? Through texts and phone calls and weekend visits when we could manage it?

Of course, it was possible. People did it all the time. But how long could Iker and I stay happy that way?

I turned up the music to drown out those depressing thoughts. Right now, I was here, and I had Iker, and that was all I could let matter.

My phone rang, and I hit the answer button on my steering wheel when I saw it was my realtor in Texas.

"Hello," I answered.

"Hi, Langley! I just wanted to let you know that I drafted offers on all three of those houses you had listed as your top choices, just like you asked."

"Perfect, thank you."

"I know you said you wanted a minute to think about which was your favorite, but I just wanted to remind you that the market is—"

"Hot right now," I interrupted. "I know. Those houses might get offers before I make my mind up, I know. I'm still going to need some time to think about it." More like, I needed some time to come to grips with the fact I'd be living eight-hundred-and-fifty miles away from the man I was falling for all over again.

"You're absolutely right!" Her reply was annoyingly chipper. "So, once you make your choice, just electronically sign the corresponding offer, and we'll be on our way!"

"Sounds great. Look, I just pulled into my apartment building, so I'll let you know when I decide, okay?"

"Perfect!"

I pulled into my numbered spot as we said our farewells and hung up. Five minutes later, I walked into my apartment with that sigh of relief that always escaped when I got home from traveling. Not that I hadn't loved growing up trotting the globe, but call me Dorothy, there was no place like home.

"Look, you're alive!" I said to my fern, noting that Iker had watered it just like he said he would. It was oddly reassuring that the guy could keep houseplants alive.

I started the shower to warm up the water, then dropped my clothes into the hamper in my room. I'd handle my suitcase later. Showering off the travel-time was an immediate necessity.

My phone buzzed as I walked into the bathroom.

Iker: Got done early. Want some company?

Langley: Hell yes, I do. I'm jumping in the shower, so use your key if I don't answer.

Without waiting for his response, I tossed my phone onto the counter and stepped under the steaming jets. I groaned in pleasure as the hot water hit my skin, then warmed my aching muscles. I wasn't addicted to much in my life, but long, hot showers were definitely my vice.

This shower was a major reason I'd rented the apartment. It was roomy, with glass walls, multiple showerheads, and a bench perfect for shaving my legs. No one liked the balancing act of one-foot-on-the-wall. By the time I'd shampooed and conditioned my hair, shaved my legs, and soaped up, my muscles were thoroughly relaxed.

"Langley?" Iker's voice came from the hall.

"In the shower!" I answered, then let my head fall back under the water to rinse the conditioner out. Damn, I'd meant to at least be in the getting-dressed phase of my post-travel routine. I didn't want to waste a single moment with Iker. "I'll be out in a second!"

"Why? I'd much rather join you."

My eyes flew open to see Iker casually leaned against my bathroom doorframe, and holy shit, if I wasn't already dripping wet from the shower, I would have been just from looking at him. Iker was in uniform.

Actual. Uniform.

I'd never been a tag-chaser. Quite the opposite, really. Guys in the military didn't do it for me, but Iker in those Multicams *definitely* did it for me. My breath caught and my skin flushed from more than the water.

We locked eyes, and his smirk faded into something so intense, I physically felt my body soften in preparation.

"Is that a yes?"

"Hmmm!" I responded, already planning my assault.

"To joining you?" he reminded me.

I nodded. He might be no-holds-barred in the bedroom, but he always made sure I was on board. It was something that cranked his sex appeal to level: Yes, please.

He made quick work of his boots, then shed his top with a rip of Velcro, never once breaking eye contact. A dull ache began between my thighs, and I cupped my breasts when they started to feel heavier.

"Do not start without me," he warned, working his belt free and dropping his camo pants.

"Then hurry," I demanded, noting with satisfaction that his eyes narrowed as I swept my thumbs over my pebbled nipples.

His t-shirt was next, followed by his underwear and socks, until he wore nothing but yards of inked, velvet skin. Three strides and he had the shower door open, then shut. Another step and his hands were in my hair and his mouth was on mine.

Welcome home.

His tongue swept in to dance with mine, and I groaned at the taste of those cool peppermints he loved against the heat of my mouth. My fingertips trailed up his sides and then down to his hips as he tilted my face to kiss me deeper. He was hard and ready against my stomach, his hips bucking when I brought my hand between us to run my thumb across his tip.

"Langley," he groaned, pressing his hand against the small of my back to bring us skin to skin from lip to thigh.

"I missed you," I admitted against his mouth.

"Same here." He kissed me deep and hard, blocking out every other thought as his hands gripped my waist.

He turned me in his arms suddenly, so my back was to his chest, then he took the lower showerhead from its mount and cranked the top until it pulsed. His lips met my neck, his teeth testing the flesh as he parted me with one hand and brought the showerhead between my thighs with the other.

"Iker!" My knees weakened at the first hit of that water against me, and he locked his forearm around my waist, hauling me back with him until he sat on the bench. Then he pulled me back onto his lap, spreading my thighs across his.

"I've thought about this since the first time I saw this shower," he growled in my ear as he brought the head back to my aching flesh. Each pulsing shot hit the area around my clit, sensitizing each nerve ending without giving me the satisfaction of pressing in on that one needy spot.

I arched back, rubbing my ass across his erection, and was rewarded by a long groan in my ear. "I need you."

"You have me."

Water still coursing over me, he slipped two fingers down my cleft until he slid them inside me. I moaned his name when he started pumping them in and out, stroking me in a rhythm that had me rocking my hips, riding those fingers.

My fingernails bit into his hips, then I put one hand in his hair and tugged him back to my neck. In this position, I had almost no control, no way to urge him to move faster.

He chuckled against my neck, but gave me what I wanted, sucking lightly where my neck met my shoulders. The water rotated, still moving, swirling, stimulating everything but my clit as his fingers fucked me with slow deliberation.

"You're killing me," I whined.

"Good, because I've been dying for you for three fucking days." He strummed his thumb over my swollen clit and I gasped.

"Iker, please!" Pleasure coiled, low and tight in my belly.

"You feel so ready for me." He added a third finger, stretching me, and my grip tightened in his hair. I could do little more than take what he was willing to give like this.

"I am. Just...please!" I begged again.

He dropped the showerhead, sending it spinning toward the drain. Then he used his fingers to stroke my clit, never ceasing the thrust of his hand, until he held me on the edge of pure madness.

My thighs locked, starting a domino effect that captured every other muscle in my body until I leaned against him, stiff and trembling. Then he finally pressed those fingers against me, the pressure sending me into a full-blown orgasm that had me shaking in his arms as it rolled through me.

Limp and sated, I sagged, my chest heaving as I sucked in steam-filled air. My hips jerked as he pulled his fingers free.

"I love feeling you do that," he growled, low and harsh in my ear.

I turned quickly, slipping my knee over so I straddled him. Then hooked my fingers through the chain of his dog tags and pulled, bringing him to me for a long, thorough kiss. His dick twitched between us, and I rose, the tile cold on my knees, and settled his tip at my entrance.

"Condom," he hissed, his eyes slamming shut as his fingers bit into my hips.

"I'm on birth control." I wanted him now, skin to skin.

"You sure?" His eyes locked on mine, his pupils flaring when I lowered myself just enough so his thick head breached me. "God, Langley."

"I'm sure." I lowered myself slowly, taking him inside me inch by delicious inch, savoring the stretch as he pushed through my rippling muscles.

"So. Fucking. Good." He managed the words between breaths as I began to ride him.

He locked one arm around my back and locked the other in my hair, tugging so my head fell back, exposing my neck to his tongue and teeth. I rose and fell in a slow, deep rhythm, swirling my hips to hear him gasp, then making us both groan when he hit the perfect spot within me.

As if he'd pressed the reset button, my body started to climb again, my muscles straining as pleasure built quickly. Before long, his breaths were ragged, and I felt him swelling within me, growing even harder. He kissed me, his tongue mimicking the movement of his hips beneath mine as he thrust up to take me deeper, harder.

It felt so damn good, I could taste it, pleasure sweet and sharp on my tongue.

"Touch yourself," he demanded, pulling my hand between us, until I felt where our bodies joined.

"Iker." I shook my head.

"Do it. I want to feel you come around me like this. God, you feel amazing." He moved my fingers beneath his, swirling over my hyper-sensitive clit.

I gasped and took over, stroking and pressing my own flesh until I tensed, unable to move as the pending orgasm held me still. Iker held the base of my neck and gripped my hip with his other hand, holding me so he could slam up into me, sending us both over the edge.

My vision blurred as pleasure swept over me in waves, then left me draped over him, my lips against his neck. It took us a few minutes to move, then another few to wash off, pausing for slow, lingering kisses.

Once we were dressed, me in shorts and a tee, him in the jeans and shirt he'd brought with him, I pulled out my laptop and set it on the kitchen counter as we started to cook dinner.

"Okay, so there are three choices," I said, pulling up all three listings.

"You're buying a house?" he questioned, pulling the pasta out of the cabinet.

"Well, yeah. It's the better financial investment." I shrugged. Rent payments would cost as much as a mortgage payment, so it made sense.

He blinked and shook his head. "Sometimes I forget that we come from two completely different worlds."

I turned and looped my arms around his waist, then rose up and brushed a kiss across his lips. "Well, I like my world way better with you in it."

"Same here," he answered with another kiss. "So, which one are you going with?"

"I thought I'd ask your opinion." I pulled up the first house. "They're all in this little suburb just north of Austin, in this cute little town. I like this one because it has a nice yard. This one has an awesome kitchen. This one has a jetted tub, which made me—Hey, are you okay?" I paused when I caught him staring at me like I had three heads.

"You want my opinion?" he asked slowly, like he'd heard wrong.

"Well, yeah. I mean, hopefully we'll be able to make weekend visits happen for both places, but I like thinking about you in all of the houses I saw." I cocked my head at him and he managed to unfurrow his brow. "Besides, two sets of eyes on something is always better than one, right?"

"It's your money."

"I know that. I just want it to feel like...I don't know. I guess I want to feel you there, like it's *ours*, so I don't miss you so much while I'm gone. I don't expect it to make sense."

He ran a hand over his hair. "I just don't want you to make a choice based on what I think, and then regret it when—"

"I'm just asking for your opinion, Iker, not a ring." I cut him off before he could finish that sentence with something stupid like, *we don't make it.*

His ears turned red, which I would have thought was cute under any other circumstances. "I get that. It's just... damn, Langley, it's a *house*. People don't just look on the Internet and order a house like it's a shirt where I come from."

I didn't remind him I'd flown down to see these houses. Instead, I stepped back and tried to see his point of view. I didn't know if his grandmother owned her house or rented. I didn't know if he ever wanted to own a house, or if he felt like one would tie him down. But I did know that the phrase, "No mortgage, I'll pay cash," wasn't something he heard often, either.

"You know what?" I said gently. "This is definitely a lot. Don't worry, I'll look at it later. Let's not worry right now." I moved to shut the laptop, but he stole it away, holding it in the palm of one hand.

"Give me a second. I just need to wrap my mind around it." He leaned back against the counter and scrolled through. Two lines appeared between his eyebrows and his eyes darted over the pictures, taking in the details and analyzing. Finally, he put the laptop on the counter and turned it so I could see.

I held my breath, unsure of what he'd say about any of it.

"Okay, not this one. See the way the patio is cracked here, and that's unlevel? It's pulling away from the foundation." He zoomed in on the picture so I could see.

"The realtor said that was fixable." I questioned her, not Iker.

"Sure, with about twenty grand in foundation repairs." He moved to the next house. "This one looks good. Plus, you're right, that yard kicks ass. I like the third one too, but the neighborhood doesn't have the best crime rating." He moved a window over in the browser, showing me the stats.

"So, the second one?" I asked.

"That's the one I would pick. You know, if I were buying a house. Which I'm not." He turned away, getting the sauce started.

"Second one, it is," I said as I pulled up the electronic offer and signed it, clicking to seal the paperwork. "Offer is confirmed. Now, we wait."

"Your life is weird," he said, but there was a smile on his lips.

"Yeah, well, it's partly your life now, too," I challenged.

"That it is, Vaughn." He leaned over and kissed me softly.

We finished up dinner without addressing the elephant in the room. I'd just put an offer in on a house in a different state, taking the first step in a move that was going to put hundreds of miles between us. This was fragile, and new, and so very wonderful, but was it flexible enough to stretch that far?

We only had weeks to make sure it was, because even if Iker lost his grip, I wasn't letting go of him this time.

Chapter 11

Iker

"**M**ake sure you plan a trip to go down and see Grandma before the summer is over."

Gael's voice was quiet, and I could tell he was reluctant to leave. We spent the last couple days arguing about my truck. He wanted me to take it back, I refused. He needed it more than I did. Plus, I needed to look at something that got better mileage since I was going to have a girlfriend who lived nearly a thousand miles away. I could already see long-ass road trips in my future.

I hooked an arm around his neck and pulled him into a tight hug. I was still getting used to the fact he was as tall as I was.

"I'll go see her. You drive safe. Text me with updates along the way." Gael had his own long-ass road trip ahead of him as he headed back to school. I was getting busier and busier at the base now that we'd been back from deployment for several weeks. The unspoken grace period was gone, so time with my brother and Langley had been limited. It sucked, since both of them were leaving.

I was used to being alone...but this was the first time in my life I was dealing with really feeling lonely. I didn't like it, not one bit.

Gael sniffed and pulled out of my hug. He rubbed his cheeks with his palms and gave me a hard look. "I'm going to be there for you, from here on out. When you leave, when you come back. I don't care if you're used to doing everything on your own, it's time you trust me to have your back. You've always had mine, now it's my turn."

I gave a jerky nod. "I'll be better at letting you in, kid." I couldn't deny coming home and having my family waiting was a nice change. I made the transition back to normal easier. It also made the bad nights less scary and insurmountable. I reached out so I could ruffle his dark hair. "Get a move on it. I've gotta run to Langley's and help her pack."

The boxes and bubble wrap filling her apartment drilled home the fact she would be gone soon. Every single time I taped a box shut, it felt like someone was squeezing my heart in a death grip.

Gael batted my hand away, his frown digging deeper into his handsome face. "Did you even try and ask her if she could stay?"

I matched him scowl for scowl as I crossed my arms over my chest. "No. I can't do that. This is her dream job." And she'd already bought a damn house. "She can't be the only one who puts in the work and makes sacrifices for our relationship. I need to do some of the heavy lifting too."

Gael's expression smoothed out and his chin dipped in acknowledgement. "That's true. If you asked her to stay and she agreed, she might resent you down the line for being the reason she gave up her dream job." He rolled his eyes at me and tossed the keys to the truck up in the air before catching them. "Leave it to you to go from never even having a girlfriend, to having one you're constantly going to have to work at keeping. You never take the easy way out."

I snorted. "Just trying to set a good example for you."

Gael chuckled. "You did. You know I'm always trying to make you proud, but I've *always* been super proud that you're my brother."

I had to clear my throat before I spoke. This kid knew exactly what to say to get right to the heart of things. "I'm always proud of you too, Gael. Head out. You're wasting daylight." Saying goodbye was hard enough. The longer we dragged it out, the tougher it got.

Gael pulled open the driver's side door. Without turning around, he tossed his final bit of advice over his shoulder. "Ask for a transfer, Iker. You've always been a top-notch soldier. You do what you're told, take your duty seriously, and have never caused the army any kind of issue. They've asked so much of you since you were just a kid. It's about time they did something for you. At the very least, put in a request. If it goes through, great. If it doesn't, you at least tried, and I'm sure Langley would appreciate the effort."

I'd been on the fence about that very thing. But, I couldn't decide if uprooting my entire life to follow a girl I'd just met, no matter how important she was, or how deep our connection ran, was romantic or certifiable. I also didn't want to get Langley's hopes up. I could ask for a transfer to a different base, but there was no guarantee it would happen, or that I'd get to stay there if I moved.

I waved at Gael, even though I doubted he was paying attention, and pulled out my phone so I could order an Uber. I needed to get on picking up a new ride sooner rather than later. Maybe I'd go for something flashy and fast this time. Naw, the weather in Colorado was super unpredictable, and the last thing I needed was a car that was garbage in the snow. However, if I did end up going to Texas... I shook my head to dispel the wayward thought. I needed to watch getting my own hopes up as well. I wanted to believe things between me and Langley would work out because we both wanted them to so desperately, but realistically, I knew we had a lot stacked against us.

I used the key she gave me to let myself into her apartment after getting dropped off. My own key, helping her pick a house, already making plans to visit her when she wasn't even gone yet—most people would say it was a little much, that we were moving too fast, but time never seemed to work for us the way it worked for other people. Langley and I were constantly caught between everything being set to fast forward, and then pause.

She was listening to some god-awful pop music, the volume loud enough she didn't respond when I called her name. I wound my way through the maze of boxes scattered on the floor, headed to the bedroom. It was the only place in the apartment she could be if she wasn't where I could see her. I stopped short outside the room when the unmistakable sounds of crying came through the partially open door.

"Langley?" I pushed through the doorway and came to an immediate halt. She was sitting on the floor, back against the bed, surrounded by a pile of books and stacks of pictures. Her face was tear-streaked, her makeup smeared and dark around her eyes. Her hair was up in a messy bun, and it was obvious she'd been in this state for quite a while. "What's wrong?"

I picked my way through the mess on her floor and lowered myself to the ground so we were sitting shoulder to shoulder. I threw my arm around her and tugged her closer. She immediately dropped her head to her shoulder and hiccupped loudly.

"I don't know how you leave everyone you love behind." She pointed at a picture of her and her father from her graduation. "It's much harder than I thought it would be. Dad is trying to be supportive, but I can tell how sad he is I won't be living right down the road anymore. It's always been just me and him against the world. I feel like I'm abandoning him, even though I know I'm not."

I ran my hand up and down her arm and kissed her on the forehead. "He's your dad. No matter what, he wants what's best for you. It'll still be you and him against the world. Distance doesn't change that." I chuckled and quipped, "On the plus side, you'll be hundreds of miles away from your wicked stepmother." I hoped she understood I was only kidding to lighten the mood.

She sniffed a little and I heard her sigh deeply. "That's true. I'm having a hard time taking the good with the bad."

I kissed her temple and told her, "It's not supposed to be easy to leave the ones you love behind."

She nodded, reaching up to twine her fingers with mine, which were dangling over her shoulder. "I really do love you, you know."

She'd said it before, usually when we were in bed and caught up in a moment. This was the first time she'd given me the words when we weren't lost in bliss and wrapped around one another.

"I know you do. You wouldn't have given me a second chance if you didn't love me. You wouldn't have worried if I was going to make it back from deployment in one piece if you didn't love me." She had a soft heart, but she'd been burned before. The only reason I got to be here with her now was because she loved me enough for the both of us while I figured my shit out. "I love you, too."

I'd been feeling that way for a long time, but this was the first time I admitted it out loud. "I've never been in love before, so I was an idiot when it came to understanding why you were so different than any other girl."

She pulled away, turning so she could look at me with huge eyes. "You love me?"

I cocked my head to the side and grinned at her. "Of course I do. You think I send a crate of pineapples to any chick who happens to cross my path?" I snorted and reached out to drag my thumb across her damp cheek. "Pineapples are reserved for the woman I love."

I let out a strangled sound when she suddenly threw her arms around my neck after crawling into my lap. She squeezed hard enough I struggled to breathe for a minute while she showered tiny kisses all over my face.

"I told myself you loved me. I reminded myself over and over again that even if you hadn't said the words, you showed me in a million different ways that you loved me. You fought for us, fixed us. I had no idea how badly I needed to hear you say it. I feel like I can breathe now."

She rested her forehead against mine and exhaled a deep breath. "Hearing you say you love me makes leaving a little bit easier."

I wrapped my arms around her waist in a loose hug and held her while she took a moment to pull herself together.

I was used to picking up and taking off at a moment's notice. I kept things in my life simple for that very reason. I felt like kicking my own ass for not considering Langley might need something more concrete from me than the reassurance I was sticking with her before she left. She joked that she wasn't asking me for a ring when we talked about the house, but maybe she should have that kind of tangible promise from me before we were separated for Lord only knows how long. I was nowhere near ready for marriage, but when I was, there was no question Langley was the one I wanted walking down the aisle toward me.

I needed to think about what I could do to show her we would be fine. But right now, I needed to get her up off the floor and get her stuff put in boxes. I was going to help her pack, make sure she had some food in her, then I was taking her to bed so I could show her, once again, how much I loved her.

I had no trouble expressing myself when it came to the physical side of our relationship. I was still learning how to give her what she needed when it came to words and emotional support.

I was never going to be the guy who was good enough for her, but she would never find anyone willing to work as hard as I would to make her happy.

Chapter 12

Langley

"I like your friends," I told Iker as he opened the door to his apartment and led me inside with a hand at my lower back.

"I'm glad, but we didn't have to spend your last night here with them." He flipped on the lights as he walked through the apartment, then headed to the kitchen.

"I'd hardly call stopping to have one beer with them after dinner spending my last night with them," I teased, walking around my overnight bag to drop my purse on the kitchen table. "Besides, I thought we agreed not to do the whole sad, mopey, last night together thing, right?"

"Right. I forgot. Beer or soda?" he asked, his head in the refrigerator. His tone was just shy of curt, which was pretty much how the whole evening had gone after he'd gotten home after work. Not that I blamed him, I was moody and on edge too.

"Soda," I answered. Driving to Austin bright and early with a hangover didn't sound like my idea of fun. Today had already been enough to drive me to drink. Saying goodbye at the shelter had been rough, and walking away from Einstein had been nearly impossible. But I had no idea what kind of hours I'd be working in Texas, and that meant I couldn't commit to caring for him. I'd stopped for lunch with my family, which equated to Camille sobbing hysterically—thank you, pregnancy hormones—and Dad choking up as he hugged me goodbye.

Not going to lie, that hit me just as hard, and I'd been in tears driving back to Iker's. Now I was the one with *his* key, since I'd officially vacated my apartment two days ago. The only thing holding me here in Colorado was Iker, and we both knew it. But my job started in less than a week, and though the papers had been signed on the house, I still had to get everything moved in and settled before starting work.

He shut the fridge and handed me a Coke, then opened his own. "I'd like to be able to remember tonight," he explained with a wry grin as he lifted his soda and leaned back against the cabinet. "Not that being drunk wouldn't help."

"I'm so sorry." I took a sip of my drink and set it on the counter opposite him.

"For what?" He pushed his sleeves up, exposing all that ink I loved to trace.

"For putting us through this." I shrugged. "For us finally having a shot and me just..." I made a gesture with my hands like a bomb, and gave him the sound effects to match. "You know, blowing it all up in our faces."

"Stop. You didn't even know I was going to ambush your life when you took that job." He swallowed and looked away. Something was itching just under his surface, and I started to wonder if maybe there was more to it than just me leaving in the morning.

"Iker, is everything okay? Other than the obvious?"

"Yep, it's all fine." He took a swig of his Coke like it was a beer, and glared at the floor.

"Please don't think that I haven't thought about turning it down at least a few dozen times." More, to be honest.

His gaze snapped to mine. "Don't go there. I know what this job means to you and your future. There's zero chance in hell I would have let you turn it down to stay here for me."

He said it with such vehemence that I blinked a few times.

"I appreciate that, but there's a part of me that's so pissed at myself." I wrapped my arms around my stomach.

"You have nothing to be pissed about." And he was staring at the wall again. Great.

"Sure, I do. Yes, this job is amazing for my future, but what if my future would be just as amazing if I chose you instead?"

His jaw locked and his hands gripped the counter so hard, his knuckles turned white.

"What if the lesson I'm supposed to be learning is that it's not the job I'm supposed to be risking everything for, it's you? It's love? Isn't that what all the songs are about? And the sappy movies? I'm supposed to start to drive away tomorrow morning, only to throw my car into park and cry that I can't go, right?"

"That shit only works out in movies, Langley. Real life doesn't happen like that. Real life is about your job, and how you provide for yourself and your family. And you know what? Real life doesn't give a shit about love. We're on our own for that." He didn't quite stomp out of the kitchen, but it wasn't his most graceful exit either.

"Iker?" I followed him into the living room, where he stood staring at three of my suitcases lined up next to the door.

"I tried," he said quietly, staring at my Samsonite like it was the enemy.

"You tried what?"

"I tried doing the big romantic thing people do at the end of movies." He tucked his thumbs into the pockets of his jeans.

"I thought showing up at graduation out of nowhere was pretty successful, plus the pineapples." I approached him like I would have a wounded tiger, knowing his claws were out and he was looking to swipe.

"That's not what I'm talking about." He sighed and shook his head. "I had my First Sergeant put in a request to branch to transfer me to Texas."

"You did?" My heart practically flew—

"It was denied. I found out this morning."

—and abruptly crashed. "Oh," I said softly. Funny how I didn't realize how badly I wanted it until it had been a possibility, even for the most remote of seconds.

"Yeah, *oh*. It appears that infantry guys are needed here, right where I already am, so there's no point moving me all the way to Texas when there's no open slot. It's all about money and the needs of the U.S. Army. We're not exactly seen as individuals at my rank."

My chest tightened as I crossed the distance between us and put myself right in front of him, staring up into those endless brown eyes. "You really did that for me? Asked to uproot your whole life just to follow me?" My voice ended on a whisper.

"It's not like I have a lot to uproot, right?" He was still focused on the suitcases behind me, anger coming off him in nearly palpable waves.

"Don't do that. Don't belittle what you've done, or the life you've made for yourself here. Your career is on the fast track, and you have phenomenal friends who care about you. The fact that you were willing to even try to move for me means more than you'll ever know." I tried my hardest, but couldn't breech that hard-as-steel wall he had up right now.

"I am totally and completely powerless in my own fucking life. I have no say in where I live, or what I do. I can't even follow the woman I love to an area with a damned army post within forty-five minutes of where she's living. Completely. Fucking. Powerless."

My mind raced. There really was a base that close. "Isn't there someone higher up that you could—"

"Do I look like the kind of guy who's going to go begging for favors?" His eyes narrowed, but at least they were finally on me. "Everything I have, I've made on my own. I've earned it. I've worked my ass off for every single tiny thing in my life, and this...Langley, I can't work for this. Being with you is the one thing I can't seem to manage, no matter how hard I fucking try. Not before, when I had to deploy, and not now, when I can't follow you. Even if there was someone I could ask a favor from, it doesn't matter. You don't get it. The army sees me as a Type One soldier, and they need Type One soldiers here at

Carson. They're all full up on Type One's at Hood. There is literally nowhere for me to go."

"Okay," I said softly.

"It's not okay! What are we going to do?" The anger stamped in every line of his expression was laced with a very real and tangible fear.

I rose on my toes, cupped his cheeks in my hands, and kissed his lips gently. Then I did it again, until he responded, his arms coming around my back. "We're going to do the same thing we were doing yesterday, Iker. We're going to talk every day, and visit as often as we can."

"You're not going to be able to take off a lot at a new job, and I only get one four-day weekend a month. That's it. And this last month has spoiled me, Vaughn. I need more time with you than a weekend a month." His forehead rested on mine, and I slid my fingers to the back of his neck, running my thumbs down the corded muscles to relieve some of his tension. "What if you decide I'm not worth it? That there's someone there who fits into your life? What if you decide we really are cursed and fall out of love with me?"

"I have that same exact fear."

He scoffed. "You are irreplaceable."

"You are, too. I missed you every single day you were gone," I told him, holding him in place when he tried to pull away. "I must have read that letter you left me at least a thousand times. The damn thing is still in my glove box."

His eyes flared.

"Yep, you can go and read it just for fun, if you like."

"I think I'll pass." A corner of his mouth lifted.

"Point is, I fell in love with you in a week, Iker. A *week*. And I fought it after you left, but it didn't matter.

142

Nothing I did worked, and even though I'd convinced myself that I was okay, I knew the minute you walked into graduation that all my healing was all a big fucking lie. I never fell back into love with you because I never stopped. I loved you for nine months across half the world, with zero contact and less than zero encouragement from you. I couldn't fucking stop. So, trust me, getting to hear your voice, and see you on FaceTime, and even get my hands on you once a month isn't a curse; it means we're incredibly lucky."

"Lucky," he repeated after I kissed him again.

"Instead of thinking about how often you can't kiss me, just think back on those nine months you were deployed."

"They sucked."

I laughed. "Yes, I know. But now think about the fact that instead of wondering what I'm doing, or who I'm kissing, and then kicking yourself for leaving me very naked and *very* willing in that hotel room, you know that I'll be in the house you helped choose, thinking about you. Missing you, and wearing the hoodie you don't yet know I've stolen from you—"

"Wait, you what?"

"And once a month, you get to kiss me. You get to make love to me. You get to know that you're the only man I could ever possibly want. Now isn't that better than not having any of it?"

His lips pursed, but he finally nodded. "I'm greedy."

I smiled, then rose on my toes and brushed my mouth over his. "Then be greedy about the time we have left, and take me to bed. Don't make me miss you before I have to."

"I can do that." He lifted me in his arms and kissed me the whole way to his bedroom with slow, deliberate, care.

He kissed me like I wasn't leaving tomorrow. Like we had days—or years—to do this. Like there was no clock or calendar, just this moment, this touch, this brush of our tongues, and this sigh.

He worked me out of my clothes and then stripped his away, and he still kept our pace unhurried. He savored every gasp as he tested his teeth along my neck, then returned to the spots that had me arching. When I reached for him, he shook his head at me and continued the onslaught of caresses, learning my curves all over again.

My back arched and my hands gripped his hair as he set his mouth over me. *Holy shit.* The things he did with his teeth and tongue were simply inhuman. Then I forgot about the suitcases and the alarm. The only thoughts in my head were *yes* and *more.* He drove into me with his tongue, then traded it for his fingers, using both to bring me to a clawing orgasm that had me chanting his name.

And once I came down from that high, he paused as he held himself above me, balanced on his elbows, my hips cradling his.

"I love you. You know that, right?" he asked, his muscles locked and straining, tiny beads of sweat manifesting on his skin from the exertion of holding back.

"I know," I said, running my fingers down the side of his cheek. "I love you, too."

He smiled, and my belly tightened at the light in his eyes and that dimple that popped out with perfect timing.

Then he slid inside me and the smiles were gone, replaced by hungry kisses and breathy moans.

He moved with power and patience, building me up again carefully with each thrust of his hips and brush of his lips, until I braced my hands against his headboard so I had better leverage. Then I gave him exactly what he was giving me, meeting him as his hips pistoned faster and harder.

"Langley, I need you with me," he growled in my ear as he slid his thumb in between us and worked my clit, spiraling that pleasure in my belly to its breaking point, until I writhed and whimpered.

Until I clenched around him as I came, and took him right over the edge with me.

This was worth working for, worth waiting for. Worth scheduling my life around. Having him in my life was worth any cost the fates demanded. I'd pay it if it meant I had his heart, his mind, and his arms.

Much later, when the clock read the early hours of the morning, I snuck out of his bed and threw on his shirt, then softly tiptoed to the kitchen. I found a pad of paper and an envelope, then sat at the table.

I wanted him to have a letter he could hold on to, one he could read and remember me by. One he could cherish the way I treasured his. I was going to pour my heart and soul out onto a piece of paper and leave it somewhere he would easily find it.

Iker,
    As I sit here writing, I wonder if this is how you
felt that morning you were the one who had to

leave. I feel gaping, empty, raw, and yet so full of everything you've given to me. I'm so heartbroken to be leaving you, and yet so thankful that it's not goodbye as much as it is a "see you later."

This is the key to our house in Texas. I say ours because that's how I'll think of us, one heart stretched across 850 miles and two homes. I want you to see this key as you walk out of this apartment every morning, and remember that it unlocks another door in another state, where I'll be dreaming of you. And yes, I'll still be dreaming because you get up entirely too early.

Maybe our lives have been too vastly different in the past, but that stops now, because we're forging a new life, one where we'll take the best parts that we love from each, and leave the bullshit behind too. We can make this whatever we want, whatever we're willing to fight for.

See these? They're the cufflinks you wore that night. Yes, I kept them. They were a reminder that you were real, and though the pain was too, you brought so much more to my life, and that was worth remembering. Worth holding on to. I'm returning them to you with the very same hands I'm using to hand you my heart. I hope they remind you that you don't just fit into my world, you shake it on its axis. No, you don't have to wear them, though I'll be the first to say that you're just as delicious in a tux as you are in jeans. But you in a uniform! Just the thought makes me want to wake you up again right now.

I love you, Iker Alvarez. I know we won't always wake up in the same bed, but I'll always wake up loving you wherever you are. Here's to our future and what we make of it.

No goodbyes.

XOXO,

Langley

"Text me when you stop for gas," Iker told me, his arms around me as he leaned back against my car door.

"I will."

"Don't speed through the little towns. Cops in small towns are assholes when you speed."

"I won't."

"Remember to take breaks. Don't get too tired, and don't be afraid to stop at a hotel if you're feeling sleepy. I'd rather know my girlfriend is alive in a random town than dead in Austin."

"Okay." I laughed softly, burying my nose in his neck. I committed everything about this moment to memory. The way he smelled, the scratch of his uniform's patches against my skin, the deep timbre of his voice rumbling through my ears and heart. My eyes prickled with tears I'd fought against shedding all morning.

"Call me if anything goes wrong." His arms squeezed tighter.

"What, so you can jump down and change a tire?" I teased.

"Don't doubt my powers, Langley Vaughn. Texas is my state, remember?" He kissed my head, and I decided not to remind him it was the second largest state in the union, thus making his claim outrageous and implausible, no matter how sweet it was.

"Okay, I'll call."

His breath was shaky as he hugged me even closer. "Don't forget to love me."

"Never." God, how was I going to do this? Drive away from him and our life? Why didn't I say no to this job? Why didn't I just take my dad up on his offer and stay here in the Springs, where I could be with Iker? Why the hell was I putting us through this?

"I'm so damned proud of you, Langley. Remember that. Every time this is hard, remember that I'm at your back. I'm in this with you, you got me?"

I tilted my head back, tears slipping from the corners of my eyes, but I managed to nod. "I got you."

Then he nodded, brushing the tears away with his thumbs. "I love you. The distance will suck, but we'll make up for it with the time we get together. I. Love. You."

"I love you," I whispered as pain took my voice right out of my throat.

"I'll see you soon. I promise. I'll drive down on my first four-day." He opened my door, and urged me into the seat.

"Promise me?" I buckled out of habit and put my hands on his clean-shaven face as he ducked into the car to kiss me again. It was sweet, lingering, and entirely too short.

"Of course," he answered with a shaky smile. "After all, you have my hoodie." He shut my door with a smirk and left me laughing like a heartbroken, lovesick idiot. Then he tapped on my hood as I started the ignition, and stood in front of my car, his arms crossed in front of his chest as I put my BMW into reverse and backed away from him.

I was still crying as I crossed the Colorado border, but I stopped by the time I reached Texas. Now I could stop counting down the moments until I left, and start counting the ones until I saw him again.

Chapter 13

Iker

" I have to give you credit, you have a lot of balls showing up here unannounced."

Langley's father was looking at me with an equal mixture of anger and concern in his gaze. The older man knew I was currently tied with him for being the most important man in his daughter's life, and Langley mentioned he had some choice words for her when she told him we were getting back together. He didn't seem to think she should bother with a long-distance relationship while trying to settle in and start a new career. He had a valid point, so I didn't take his opinion personally. I did, however, hesitate when it came to approaching him because Langley let me know her father knew about our deal for the wedding, and the money.

It was embarrassing to have my girlfriend's father be privy to one of the lowest points and worst decisions I'd ever made. I knew the complicated past between me and Langley was enough to make this man question if I had the best intentions when it came to his daughter.

Which was why I'd shown up at his office out of the blue. I was worried he would refuse to see me if I tried to schedule something ahead of time. I figured a surprise attack would work in my favor. It'd gotten me in the door and a cool, but not hostile, reception.

I twisted my uniform cap around in my hands and cleared my throat. "I'm here because of Langley."

Because I could tell she was crying every time we talked on the phone.

Because she looked like she wasn't sleeping at all whenever we FaceTimed.

Because she was so caught up in missing me and Colorado, she was letting new experiences and amazing opportunities slip right by her.

She'd been gone for two months, and I'd made the trip down there once, but I swore adjusting to the distance and change in our relationship had been the hardest thing I'd ever done...and I'd been in combat in more than one warzone.

"I know when I ask you what I'm about to ask you, you're going to think it's for me, that I'm being selfish and problematic, but I wouldn't ask, couldn't bring myself to beg, if it wasn't for your daughter." I sighed and lowered my eyes to where my knee was bouncing up and down. "I'm really worried about her. I don't want her to give up on the job and her future before she's given herself a chance to succeed."

The older man laced his fingers together and placed them under his chin. "I heard through the grapevine you asked for a transfer before Langley left, and that it was denied."

I lifted a shoulder and let it fall. "Asking was the least I could do."

And as such, it was why I was here now, ready to plead my case for all I was worth. It was clear I couldn't fix things the way I promised on my own. I needed help, but I had no clue if the man across from me was willing. He probably had lofty expectations for whoever he deemed good enough for his daughter. I was sure I came up lacking on all fronts, but I had to exhaust every avenue possible to keep Langley's dream on track. She was out of control right now, and the last thing I wanted to do was stand by, helpless, while she crashed and burned.

"You're really worried about her, aren't you?" Mr. Vaughn dropped his hands and leaned forward, placing them on the desk in front of him.

I nodded and told him in all seriousness, "I am. I spent my whole life trying to get out of Texas. I only go back to visit my grandmother. I never gave much thought to going back until Langley told me she was moving. Now, I don't care where I live as long as I get to have a life with her when I'm home. I'm supposed to be the guy who takes care of her forever, and I can't do that from this far away."

Her father grunted and lifted his silvery eyebrows. "Do you think you've earned the right to take care of her? She was heartbroken when you left last time. I hated seeing her cry herself to sleep every single night. You were lucky you deployed. If you'd been in town, I would have had to track you down and teach you some manners."

I brushed my hand over my hair and forced myself to meet his probing gaze. "I screwed up. I knew as soon as I walked out the door. I will spend every minute of every day trying to make it up to Langley." Again, that task would be much easier if I could close some of the distance between the two of us.

"What about the money? Ten grand isn't pocket change. How do I know you won't do something else drastic and reckless if you end up in another financial bind? How do I know you won't hurt my daughter if you get desperate again?" He rapped his knuckles on the desk and stared at me unflinchingly.

"I would do anything for my little brother. That will never change. I'm sure you know that Langley already provided a scholarship for a couple students to finish school. My brother was one of them, because Langley bailed me out when his financial aid fell through at the last minute. I won't ever find myself in that kind of situation again." I shifted on the leather wingback chair and pulled a well-worn check out of my pocket. Leaning forward, I placed it on the desk. "I tried to give Langley the ten grand back. I wanted her to know it was a loan, not me taking advantage of her. She refused to accept it. Take the check. Put it one of her retirement accounts or something." I doubted she would ever notice, and the slate would finally be wiped totally clean.

Mr. Vaughn reached out and slid the check across his desk with his index finger. "I wasn't expecting that. You're full of surprises, aren't you, young man?"

"I just want to do right by your daughter, sir." I lifted a hand so I could rub the back of my neck. "I won't sit here and say I deserve any kind of preferential treatment. Maybe I haven't done enough, proved my worth, but Langley has. She has the best heart of anyone I've ever met. She's selfless and kind. She deserves the best. So, this is me, trying to show you I'm what's best for her."

A heavy silence fell between us as the older man continued to watch me with sharp eyes. Eventually, Mr. Vaughn tapped a finger on the check and gave me a strained grin.

"She's not as selfless as you might think. She doesn't ever ask for anything, but when she does, it's for something big and hugely important." He tilted his head to the side slightly and the grin fell away. "She called me the first week she was gone and asked if there was anything I could do to push a transfer for you through. I know people who know people, and there are some powerful men on Carson who owe me more than one favor."

He grunted and gave his head a little shake. "You're right in being worried about her. She's putting on a brave face, but she isn't doing well. She jumped into the deep end, and it's taking everything she has to tread water. If she's handling things this poorly, when you can get on a plane and fly to Austin anytime you want, how do you think she's going to handle it when you're gone for months on end without any way to contact her? I don't know if sending you down there will help or hurt her, if I'm being honest."

I had the same thought more than once, but all we could do was cross that bridge when we came to it. I was also not surprised in the least she'd already tried to pull some strings in order to end both our suffering.

"All I know is that things can't go on like they are. She's miserable, and every time I hear or see her cry, I'm tempted to go AWOL. Either I'm going to do something

154

stupid to get to her, or she's going to bail on everything and eventually, she'll resent what she had to give up, and me. She'll start thinking about all the people she could've helped if she stuck it out. I don't want her to live with regret. I spent nine months in the desert, consumed with doubt and remorse over leaving Langley the way I did. All I could think about was how different things might have been if we had a chance. I'll do whatever it takes to give her her chance."

If he wanted me on my knees, pleading and praying, I would do it. Not for anyone or anything other than Langley. For her, there wasn't a single thing I could think of I wouldn't do.

Mr. Vaughn climbed to his feet and started to pace behind his desk. "What if moving to Texas to give Langley her chance doesn't work out in your favor? What if you have to lose a rank? What if the two of you break up and you're stuck in a state you said yourself you didn't want to return to? Giving Langley her chance very well might mean you lose yours when it comes to advancement. Have you considered any of those things?"

I had. Maybe I couldn't lose rank, but I could lose squad leader time, which would hurt me for the E-7 promotion list. I also decided none of it mattered in the long run. "I'm looking at a lifetime spent in the military, sir. If I take a step back right now, there isn't much stopping me from taking ten forward as the years go on. I'll be okay, wherever I end up and with whatever happens to me. I'm not so sure the same can be said for your daughter."

He nodded. "That's a good answer. All any father wants to know is how much the man who is in love with his daughter is willing to sacrifice."

I'd give up everything if I had to.

"I told Langley I couldn't call in a favor of that magnitude just because she missed her boyfriend. I told her if you were the one who approached me, if you came and asked me personally to intervene on your behalf, I would consider it after hearing what you had to say. I didn't think you could convince me helping you transfer to Texas was the right move." Once again, he knocked his knuckles on the desk. "You proved me wrong. It's clear you've thought through all the plus and minuses. It is also clear you are putting Langley first."

I gulped and wiped my suddenly sweaty hands on my pants. It felt like everything was on the line, and the tension was thick enough to choke on.

"I've never been the type of person comfortable asking for a favor or a handout. I make my own way, and I take care of my own, on my own." I didn't love hearing that Langley already pleaded our case to her father, but I gave her some leeway since I knew how much she was struggling. I told Langley I would fix things, and in order to do so, I needed help. In a fight for survival, I was trained to use whatever advantage I could in order to come out on top. Corbin Vaughn was merely a tool to get the outcome I wanted. I could barely feel the sting of my pride burning under my skin.

"You're well on your way to being family, Iker. I'd like to think eventually you'll be comfortable relying on me. Ultimately, we both want my daughter to be happy. That makes us allies, not enemies. I'll make some calls, press some buttons, and see if I can get your transfer request looked at again. I obviously can't promise anything."

I jumped to my feet and reached out to shake his hand. He gave my fingers a tight squeeze and lifted his eyebrows as he asked, "Want to ask my permission to marry her while you're in the process of requesting the impossible for her already?"

I balked and must've paled because Mr. Vaughn tossed his head back and let out a loud belly laugh.

"I'm kidding. I'm glad you aren't rushing into marriage. Though, I did propose to Langley's mother after only knowing her for three weeks. Sometimes you just know when it's right." He clapped a hand on my shoulder and gave me a little shake. "I do expect you to talk to me before you decide to take that step."

I nodded like a bobblehead doll. "I will, but I gotta tell you, there is no way in hell our wedding will be anything like that fiasco you had for your stepdaughter." No way. No how.

Langley's father chuckled. "Fair enough." He waved a hand in the direction of his office door. "Cross your fingers. I'll be in touch when I have more information. Try and keep Langley afloat the best you can."

I swore to do my best and slipped out the door, shaking more than I had when I walked in. I couldn't believe he hadn't turned me away and told me to suck it up. He was so nice and sincere, it was easy to see where Langley got her compassion and empathy from. I couldn't believe he so readily accepted me into their affluent family. He didn't look at me like I was an interloper at all, and I didn't want to be all sappy and emotional, but it had been kind of cool to be on the receiving end of authentic fatherly advice for once in my life.

Growing up without either of my parents around, I'd missed out on moments like that, and instead had to fill the role for my brother. The Vaughns brought so much into my life. I would be eternally grateful they were so forgiving.

For the first time since she drove away, I felt a small spark of hope start to glow in the center of my chest. I didn't want to get my expectations up too high...because the crash back down to Earth would be devastating. Instead, I planned to keep my fingers crossed like Mr. Vaughn suggested, and put as much good luck and good will as I could muster out into the universe, in the hopes I might get paid back tenfold.

Chapter 14

Langley

I blinked as the numbers in the financial report on my desk began blurring together. Late hours had become my norm, not just because there was so much work to be done, but because throwing myself into work was the ultimate coping mechanism.

"Hey, Langley, don't stay too late, okay?" Jessica Hallstrom said from my office doorway.

I glanced at the corner of my computer. "It's only six, no worries."

"It was only eight more than a few times this week," she chided. "I love your enthusiasm, and we're lucky to have you, but you're going to burn out if you keep this up. Now, go home and get some rest. That's a direct request from your boss." She gave me an understanding smile.

I gave the next fund's analytics a longing look.

"Oh no, you don't. I'm waiting right here until you walk out with me." She crossed her arms, her purse already over one shoulder. "And no taking work home, either."

Well, shit. Grumbling, I shut down my computer and abandoned the few files I had on my desk. It was nothing that couldn't wait until Monday.

"So, I moved here from Maryland," Jessica told me as we rode the elevator to the parking garage beneath our high-rise office building.

"Really?" Given the soft drawl she had when she pronounced some words, I hadn't caught on.

"Yep. Moved here a little over ten years ago, straight out of college. That transition was awful. I missed my friends and my family all of the time." She looked at me meaningfully.

"It's been rough," I admitted. "I miss my family and my boyfriend."

"That's normal. So is spending long weekends back in Colorado. I get it. I just want you to know that it will get easier. You'll adjust in little ways until one day, you'll realize you have your feet under you." The elevator dinged at the P1 level and we walked into the garage. "When is the next visit with your boyfriend?"

"Two weeks," I answered instantly. The date was marked on the calendar with a big red circle. "We missed last month because he was in the field, so it's been a while." A while was an understatement. By the time Iker's feet touched Texas soil, it would have been close to two months since I'd seen him last.

The army threw a whole different wrench into our relationship. Not only were we struggling to find long weekends to make the trip, but then he'd leave for a month with his unit for training and it didn't even matter if I splurged on an airplane ticket for a normal weekend—

he wasn't there anyway. He'd gotten back a couple of weeks ago, but when I tried to head up to the Springs this weekend, he'd told me he was going to be in the field again.

"That's got to be hard." Her expression softened. "You know, if you ever need some time, we can make it happen so you can get back there more often. God knows you work enough overtime to more than earn you a few three-day weekends."

"Thank you. I really appreciate it. I just don't want to take advantage of you or this job. Doing what I love has been so rewarding," I told her as I reached my car, noting with more than a little sadness that it boasted Texas plates instead of my pretty, green, Colorado ones. Such a stupid little thing to get me down, but it was one more piece of me—or rather my car, I guess—the move had cost me.

"You're good at it." She and I both opened our driver's doors, looking at each other over the tops of our cars. "You're already making a difference in the two funds you've been analyzing and adjusting, and I can't wait to see the quarterly returns. I'd be interested in your suggestions about where to move some of those profits. We already support a wide variety of charities, but I know I tend to get super invested in a fund when I know it's benefiting one of my personal passions."

"Thank you! I'll prepare some thoughts." And *that* made it all worth it. No matter how much I missed Iker, I was doing some real good here, and that felt amazing.

"Perfect. Now get home and relax this weekend." Jessica gave me a wave, and we both headed home.

The drive was pretty easy, twenty-five minutes or so during Friday rush hour. I could have cut down my commute and bought a condo in Austin, or a house a little closer, but I loved the small-town atmosphere where I'd bought my house. Besides, I could be just as lonely in Austin as I was at my own house. It was all the same when I came home to an empty house.

I pulled into the driveway, already mentally going through my rotating list of takeout options, and hit the garage door opening. The damned thing didn't budge.

"What the hell?" I muttered, pressing the button again. Then I put the car in park and hopped out, walking over to the numeric panel at the door. I punched in my code and it didn't even try to lift. Not a single sound.

The joys of owning a home seemed to be endless. "No big deal," I reminded myself as I grabbed my purse from my passenger seat, then closed and locked my door. "Probably just need to reset a breaker, or something."

Had to admit, I was still getting used to being on my own when things went wrong. Iker fixed the dishwasher, but that was because it had broken when he was here for his first visit and he told me not to spend money on something he could handle.

I walked the path to my front door, then unlocked it and walked in. A sigh of relief tumbled past my lips as my heels hit the hardwood in the small entry.

"Honey, I'm home," I called out sarcastically as I turned the corner into the kitchen, then stilled. My sliding glass door to the backyard was open. There was no way in hell I'd left it open this morning. I was way too paranoid for that.

Before I could get my cell phone free to dial 911, a white cloud of fluff raced through the opening, heading straight for me.

I gasped and fell to my knees as Einstein jumped, his paws landing on my shoulders with an excited yap before he licked my face up the side. "Oh my God! Hiya, Einstein! What are you doing here? I missed you!" I word-vomited all over the dog.

"He missed you, too."

My eyes squeezed shut at the sound of his voice and I held Einstein to me, scared to look, to see that my work hours had finally taken their toll and this was all a big, fat hallucination.

"Baby, open your eyes."

The voice was even closer, and I slowly raised my lids.

Iker stood in the doorway, dressed in Multicams and an incredible smile. He was here. In my house—our house—in Texas.

"I thought you were in the field this weekend?" My voice sounded strange in my own ears. Probably because my throat was closing with alarming quickness.

"Yeah, so I might have lied to you, just a little." He cringed, but walked closer, holding out his hand. "Any chance I might be able to get one of those hugs you're giving away down there?"

I set Einstein down and Iker took my hand, pulling me straight from the floor and into his arms. Mine flew around his neck, and I breathed in the unique scent that was pure Iker. With the first inhale, my stress level dropped about a bajillion points and my heart rate jumped. His arms locked around my back, lifting me high against him.

"What are you doing here?" I asked against the skin of his neck. "Don't answer that. I don't even care. I'm just so glad you're here."

"It had almost been two months," he explained. "I couldn't take it another day. God, I missed you, Langley."

"I missed you," I agreed, finally pulling back enough to see his face. His skin was tanned, no doubt due to the month he'd just spent at the National Training Center in California. "You look so good." I grinned. "Then again, I missed you so much that you could turn up looking half-dead and I'd probably jump you anyway."

His dimple popped. "I almost forgot how good it feels to hold you."

"Almost?" I teased.

"You're burned on my brain, but on the days when I miss you so much, I can barely breathe? Yeah, then I almost forget what it feels like to have you under my hands. But, I will never forget how you taste." He lowered his mouth to mine and kissed me sweetly at first, just the press of our lips and mingled breaths, before he touched the tip of his tongue to the seam of my lips, and I opened on reflex. Then the kiss turned into something hot, wild, and utterly abandoned.

My ass hit the kitchen counter and then his hand was in my hair, twisting in the strands as his mouth took mine and brought me home. Our tongues tangled and stroked, and just like that, it was as if we hadn't been apart for months. We were simply...us. My skirt slipped to my hips, and since I never wore hose in the Texas heat, that left only a couple layers between us.

The sound of lapping water distracted me.

"Okay, wait," I said as I found an ounce of common sense. "The shelter let you bring Einstein?" I looked over to see him happily drinking out of a ceramic dog bowl Iker must have brought with him.

"Well, yeah, since I adopted him." He shrugged, but his eyes lit up.

"You what?" My mouth fell open.

His eyes dropped to my lips. "I adopted him." Then he kissed me again and I got lost in the feel of his lips against mine. Somehow, being separated so often made every kiss feel like the first one in the best way.

"Hold up." I pushed at his chest. "How did you adopt him? You're gone so often!"

"Yeah, but I came up with a great family care plan," he teased, referring to the form soldiers had to fill out regarding their very human kids.

"Oh, really?" My hands rested on his uniform and my brow puckered. "And why are you in uniform? Not that I'm complaining because you know how I feel about you in uniform." It was the only time he wore dog tags, and man, did I like to use those to pull him closer.

"What can I say? I was so excited to get to you that I just couldn't wait to change into civies." That grin was back, but when he ducked his mouth toward mine, I evaded.

"Oh no, you don't. I have questions, and your kisses muddle my brain." I narrowed my eyes at his handsome face, sighing in pure feminine appreciation at his strong jaw and full lips. "All of you muddles me." I shook my head. "Let me get this straight. You stopped by your house, picked up Einstein that you adopted..." I raised my eyebrows in question.

"Yesterday," he answered.

"Right. Yesterday. So, you picked up Einstein, then didn't change, and then, what? Hopped the first flight?

165

Did you take a half-day?" Even though my body was screaming out its need for me to shut up and jump Iker, my brain had way too many questions.

"I drove, actually." He ran his hand down my hair, gathering a strand of the long, blonde stuff and rubbing it between his thumb and forefinger with a smile.

"Wait, what? I didn't see your car—" My eyes popped wide. "You disconnected the garage door!"

"I wanted to surprise you." He grinned again, and I was powerless as he swept me into another kiss that had my hands clutching the fabric of his uniform and my thighs gripping his hips.

"And you drove thirteen hours in uniform?" I managed to say as his lips trailed a path down my neck, sending shocks of *yes, please* straight to my belly.

"No. I changed when I got here." He followed my neckline and then kissed my collarbone.

"You what?" I leaned back on my palms, putting as much distance between us as I could without unlocking my ankles. "You left at, what? Three a.m.? Then drove here and put *on* your uniform?" This made absolutely no sense. Iker was never in uniform unless he was going to or leaving work.

"You're really preoccupied with the uniform," he said, unzipping his top and throwing it to the opposite counter. His shirt was next, leaving him deliciously bare-chested.

"Huh." My breath caught, and I felt that rush of wet between my thighs that always happened when those abs came out to play. He might as well have pressed a button that said, "Push here to prep Langley."

"Is that better?" he asked, that sly, smoldering smirk redirecting my attention.

"Mmmm. So good." My fingers drifted from his chest to his beltline. God, the man was all hard edges wrapped in warm, smooth skin. "Wait. No! Stop distracting me, Iker Alvarez!"

"I'm sorry. What else were you asking?" He was always happy when we were together, but that grin was off the freaking charts today.

"Why would you put *on* your uniform? Just because I like it? Because I'm down with that, but it seems like a lot of work to go through."

"Well, I couldn't report to Fort Hood in civies." He raised both eyebrows.

Mine bunched together. "Why would you report? Is your unit here?" A flash of excitement smacked me in the chest. "Iker, is your unit training here?"

His thumb brushed my lower lip. "Yes, my unit trains here."

"For how long?" Oh my God, maybe I'd get him for a couple of weeks!

"Forever," he answered softly, watching me with an intensity that had me blinking.

"Forever?" I repeated, my heart clenching.

He nodded, a slow smile spreading across his face.

"What are you trying to tell me?" Now my heart was pounding, slamming against my ribs so hard I was sure he had to be able to hear it.

"I got the transfer. It was a pretty behind-the-scenes thing, so it happened quickly."

"You live here?" I whispered as chills raced down my spine.

"As of today, I do."

We stared at each other, my mouth agape and eyes wide, his features slowly transforming from excited to schooled.

"Langley, say something. This is what you wanted, right?" When he would have stepped away, I kept my ankles locked and flexed my thighs.

"More than anything," I admitted. "I'm just scared to believe it. How? When? Do you have to go back? Does your family know?" The questions flew from my lips.

His smile flashed and his shoulders dipped in relief. "When? Now. I found out on Monday afternoon and broke my lease. Tuesday and Wednesday, I put basically everything I owned up on Craigslist and cleared Fort Carson, which is pretty much the fastest clearing any paperwork pusher has ever seen. Thursday, I rented a U-HAUL and packed, and I left this morning around one a.m."

"So, you're here? You live here. Like...go to work here, and come home here?" I sat up fully, resting my hands on his waist.

"Well, I'm hoping you'll let me come home here. If you think it's too fast to move in together, I can get a place closer to base, but it's only about a forty-minute drive so it's not too bad—"

I shut his mouth with mine, kissing him with abandon. My nails grazed his scalp, my hips rocked into his, and he—

"Hold up." He managed between ragged breaths. Great, now he was the one putting on the brakes. "The *how* was your dad."

"My dad?" Want to kill a girl's sex drive? Just mention her father while you're between her thighs.

"I went to him about a month ago and asked him to help me. To help us." He rested his forehead against mine. "Your old man came through."

My face crumpled and my nose stung with the tears I knew were about to hit. "You asked him for help?"

He nodded. "I couldn't do it anymore. You being here. Me there. You were miserable and I was a wreck. I'm into you too deep to live eight hundred miles away from you. I need this smile every day." He ran the back of his hand along my cheek.

"I can't believe you went to him. I know it sounds so freaking silly, but I'm proud of you, Iker." Asking my dad for help was up there on a list of things he'd probably rather cut off his own arm than do.

His mouth tightened. "My pride doesn't exist when it comes to you, Vaughn. I'll do whatever it takes to be near you."

"Thank you," I whispered, brushing a kiss across his lips. My dad promised he'd try to help him if Iker asked—he played golf with the commanding general of Fort Carson, for God's sake, but said Iker had to be the one to step up and do the asking.

"You don't have to thank me. Especially when the motivation is pretty damn selfish. I breathe better when I'm with you."

"Oh my God. Of course, you're living here," I blurted, his earlier words finally sinking in. "If there's anything the past months have taught me, it's that I'm not wasting a single minute that I can be with you. Even forty minutes away is too far."

"Thank God, because everything I own is sitting in your garage." He laughed.

"Our garage," I reminded him with a kiss. "And you brought Einstein! You adopted him, for me. I can't believe you!"

"Yeah, and it was a good thing I had you as a personal reference. Then again, the ten-thousand-dollar donation I gave them probably didn't hurt." He shrugged.

"You didn't." The man freaking *shrugged* at donating ten grand.

"I did." His expression turned serious. "I wasn't bringing that part of our past here, Langley. This is a fresh start. I get that you own the house, and trust me, we're about to have a huge discussion on me paying the bills because there's zero chance I'm letting you foot the bill on everything." He put his finger across my lips when I tried to interrupt him. "That money is gone. I'm here. This is where we build our future."

"Okay," I answered softly.

"Okay?" His eyes narrowed.

"You said you had no pride where I'm concerned. I have no stipulations where you are. No rules, no boundaries. We'll figure it out together."

"Together," he repeated with a soft kiss on my forehead. "I love the sound of that."

"Good, because there are so many things we're about to do together. Starting upstairs in that very big bed you made me buy." I grinned.

"Hey, all I said was that there was more room for maneuvers in a king-size." He pulled me forward and lifted me, supporting my ass with his hands.

"Time to put your money where your mouth is," I challenged, wrapping my arms around his neck. It was insane to think this had all started with a ten-thousand-dollar deal, and now it was beginning all over in the best of ways.

"You're on," he answered, stealing my breath with a series of kisses that left me mindless with pure physical need.

Then he showed me those maneuvers.

And more than a few others.

Epilogue

Iker
~ One year later

"I can't believe they put us in the same room. What are the odds?"

I could hear the amazement in Langley's voice, and I was glad I was in front of her, because I doubted I could keep a straight face. The odds were slim we'd end up in the exact same room we'd stayed in at the Broadmoor for her stepsister's wedding. I had to reserve the stupid thing months in advance and run interference when she asked pointed questions about our trip back to the Springs for her niece's first birthday.

"It must be fate." I glanced over my shoulder in her direction, pleased to see a bright smile on her face.

"What if I cry? I have good and bad memories of that room." She poked me in the side. "No making fun of me if I get emotional."

Oh...she was going to get emotional all right. I could only hope those feelings fell on the joyful side of the fence instead of the side that held the devastation from the night I left her alone in the king-sized bed. I was hoping what I had planned would wipe all those bad memories from her mind for good.

"When do your grandmother and Gael get into town?" Langley reached out and hooked her hand in the crook of my elbow. "My dad is very excited to finally meet your family."

"Grandma gets in tomorrow morning. Gael will be here sometime tonight." I was still incredibly leery about having our families co-mingle, knowing my abuela wouldn't stand by quietly and take Virginia Vaughn's shit. Especially since the older woman loved Langley like her own. She wouldn't stay quiet if Langley's wicked stepmother crossed the line. I'd like to say the rich bitch's wrath had quieted with time and space, but she only seemed to get more bitter, angry, and greedy as time went on. I had no idea how Mr. Vaughn put up with the awful woman, but they did say love was blind. I was sure Langley got her fair share of criticism and questions for being with a guy like me.

Langley and I had taken to driving down to my hometown at least once a month so we could spend time with my grandmother. The two women instantly connected, and now I was stuck trying to convince my grandmother to move closer to us so we could help her out more and keep an eye on her as she got older. She was resistant, but let it slip if Langley and I decided to have kids down the road, and if we stayed in Austin, she would consider it. Talk about playing hardball.

"I haven't seen Gael in forever. I'm so glad he agreed to come." She rested her head on my shoulder and I could feel her giddy excitement. "I bet he's taller than you now."

I snorted because she was right. My little brother hit a late growth spurt and now had a solid two to three inches on me. "Doesn't matter. I can still take him." Gael would always be more of a lover than a fighter, no matter how big he became.

"I'm surprised he took time off work to fly out for a baby's birthday party." Langley squeezed my arm as we reached the door to the opulent hotel room. "He's been so busy."

He was busy. He was taking summer classes and working a part-time job, as well as tutoring other students. There was no way in hell he would make time for an over-the-top birthday party for a toddler, but he would always make time for me and Langley.

"It's been a minute since he saw Grandma, and I think he was worried about her meeting your family for the first time. He's coming as reinforcements."

She smacked my stomach. "My family isn't that bad."

I chuckled and flashed the card for the door over the sensor. "No, he's coming to keep Grandma in check. She likes you, so she's always nice. When you cross her..." I shook my head. "Why do you think I kept myself on the straight and narrow when I was growing up? She's scary."

Langley rolled her eyes at me and moved into the room when I put a hand on her lower back. She started to ask me something, but her voice trailed off as we made our way deeper into the room. It was still as fancy and over the top as I remembered from our first time here, but now, the room was filled with those damn lilies Langley loved, and hundreds of balloons.

She stumbled to a halt, head whipping around to look at me and then swinging back around to take in the silvery, shimmery balloons spelling out W-I-L-L Y-O-U M-A-R-R-Y M-E. There was even a massive, inflated ring balloon with a big ol' balloon diamond on it. The whole setup was a little cheesy, but I knew it was all right up Langley's alley. There was a hint of nostalgia and whimsy to the whole thing I figured she'd appreciate.

Pulling out the ring, which had been burning a hole in my pocket for the better part of six months, I got on one knee and waited for her to turn and face me. When she did, her eyes were glassy with tears and her fingers were covering her mouth.

"Iker?" She sounded breathless, and she even swayed on her feet slightly.

"Will you marry me, Langley?" If she said yes, I'd tell her I already asked her old man for her hand. If she said yes, I would tell her this moment was the most important one in my life. If she said yes, I would promise her a lifetime of good memories so she always had enough to overshadow the bad.

If she said yes...I would be the happiest man alive.

"I know we've had our ups and downs." The last year had been all about growing together and adapting to being two parts of a whole.

I'd needed to work on asking for input instead of always moving forward full-steam ahead, like I'd always done. Langley needed to adjust to the fact she often had to share me with the army. Even though we lived together, she still ended up on her own a lot, which meant building a fulfilling and flourishing life outside of our relationship.

We'd had a pregnancy scare a few months into our living together. The idea of having a baby with her wasn't nearly as frightening as I thought it would be, but like everything else in our relationship, the timing wasn't right. The incident brought us closer together and taught us how to communicate more clearly when important issues came up.

Einstein got out one day, and Langley was devastated. Seeing her heart break for the dog she loved like a child, I knew I would always try my best to make sure she never hurt that way again. Luckily, the little mutt turned up at a neighbor's house, unharmed, but the ordeal was a good reminder I needed to be careful with Langley's heart because it was fragile and delicate.

"But I wouldn't trade a single good or bad moment. I love all the moments we get to spend together. I don't think I was living my life for myself until I met you. You are the first, and last, woman I've ever wanted to keep. You are the only one I will ever ask to wait for me. I want to marry you, have kids with you, be with you. I want you, forever." I held out the ring and watched as tears spilled over her long eyelashes.

"I... Are you serious right now?!" She tossed back her head and started laughing. Tears and laughter at the same time. I knew she was going to be emotional, but not that she was going to glitch. "Of course I'll marry you. I can't wait to be your wife."

She held out her hand so I could slide the simple, solitaire diamond on her finger. Classy. Pretty. Understated. Flawless. The ring was all the things she was. It looked like it belonged on her hand. Once the bauble was in place, she let out a victory shriek and threw herself at me, taking me down to the ground since I was only balanced on one knee.

"This is why your family is coming to Colorado, isn't it? I knew there was no way you would invite them to that stupid birthday party. *You* didn't even want to come." She dropped tiny kisses all over my face, stopping to give me a real kiss when she got to my mouth. "I'm so happy right now. This proposal was perfect."

I wrapped my arms around her as we lay sprawled on the floor. The hem of her sundress rode up, and we had landed with all my favorite parts perfectly aligned. The proposal was almost perfect. There was still one thing I needed to do to set everything back to rights.

"I want to take you to bed. I want to spend all day and all night making love to you, Langley. And then, when you wake up in the morning, I want you to know I'm still beside you. I'll always be there, right next to you." Sometimes I couldn't be there physically, but I would be there in spirit, always. "This time, I'm staying. Wild horses couldn't drag me away." No, only the army could do that.

She smiled down at me, reaching out a finger so she could trace the line of my eyebrows. "Sounds good." She lowered her head and dropped a sweet little kiss on the end of my nose. "Let's save the bed for later, though."

She put her hands on my shoulders and pushed herself up, so she was straddling my hips. Her hair fell in a shimmery gold wave around her shoulders, and her smile was bright enough to light up the darkest places inside of me. She watched me with mischievous eyes as she slowly slid the straps to her dress off her shoulders and down her arms. "I'm impatient. I can't wait to make love to my fiancé."

Holy shit.

I was someone's fiancé.

I was going to be someone's husband.

And chances were, I would eventually be someone's father.

Whose life was this? I'd gone from being chronically alone, to having so many important people filling up my days. I couldn't remember the last time I was lonely, and that was such an amazing feeling.

I let her tug my shirt up and over my head. I stayed mostly still as she wrestled with my belt buckle and the fastening of my jeans. I didn't manage to remain compliant when the front of her dress dropped down and I caught a glimpse of her pert, pink nipples poking against the lace of her strapless bra. Muttering my approval of her quick hands and even faster tongue as she licked her way up my throat, I grabbed a handful of her dress and tugged the fabric upward until I could get my hands on her underwear. The lacy material matched her bra, because she always matched, and was super delicate. I knew from experience most of her undergarments tended to be expensive, but flimsy. All it took was a twist and swift jerk of the wrist to tear them off of her. I'd add this set to the running list of ones I needed to replace.

Langley moaned and dragged her nails down my ribs. Goose bumps lifted across my skin, and my hips shifted under her weight when I felt her already-damp center press against the tight muscles of my lower abdomen. Her teeth locked down on the spot where my pulse started to hammer at the base of my throat, and her fingers skated across my abs and down the length of my happy trail until they wrapped around the base of my rigid cock.

Langley's teeth nipped at my earlobe and she giggled. The sound shot desire, hot and sharp, all the way through my body. She kissed her way across my jawline while her hands stayed busy stroking and sliding up the length of my now throbbing and aching cock. Her lips landed on mine, tongue immediately demanding entrance.

While she was distracted, licking and nipping at my mouth, I got my hands on her breasts, fingers plucking at her nipples hidden behind the lace. The dual sensation of my hands and the intricate pattern of the lace must have been a sensation overload, because she immediately moaned into my mouth and started to shift and grind where she was sitting on top of me.

Who knew getting engaged was such an aphrodisiac? Our sex life was never lacking, but there was something special about being with the person you officially belonged to, and the one whom officially belonged to you. Not the creepy, possessive way, but in the heart and soul kind of way. In the "your heart wasn't whole without them" kind of way.

It was hot. Both of us tangled together, half-dressed and impatient on the floor. I liked the way she writhed on top of me, and she liked the way I rocked up against her silky, soft folds, dragging the tip of my eager dick through the moisture already dotting my skin and the inside of her thighs. This was going to be fast and messy.

I couldn't wait.

She kissed me breathless, hands braced above my head as she rocked her hips to meet the slow press of my cock into her sweet opening. Her eyes glittered down at me, the love she felt clear as day.

She sat up, her body sinking down fully on mine. We both gasped as pleasure sparked and swirled around us. The atmosphere got heady and sensual as she started to glide in a sexy rhythm, our bodies always seeming to be in sync. She moved her hands so they cupped her breasts. I watched with avid eyes as her fingers started to pluck and play with her nipples.

So hot.

And so was that velvety place between her legs where we were joined. She threw her head back and closed her eyes when I snaked a hand between us, blindly searching for the little bundle of nerves that was guaranteed to make her go crazy. Her eyes widened, her mouth opened, and her hands stilled where she was touching herself. She whispered my name and started to rotate her hips in erratic circles. The back of my knuckles brushed against my erection, dragging through the wetness coating the stiff flesh.

It was a lot of sensation and a lot of emotion.

It was so much goodness I would never understand how a guy like me deserved any of it.

I would never get used to the fact that I got to touch Langley like this.

I would never get tired of hearing the way she said my name, like she was asking for both forgiveness and punishment in the same breath.

And I would never, ever forget the way she looked when she put my ring on, and then made love to me on the floor of the hotel room that held our best and worst memories.

We hit our completion within moments of one another. She whispered that she loved me, and I told her she was my everything.

That was it.

She. Was. Everything.

And I... Well, I was a boy in love.

The End

Acknowledgements

First and foremost, I want to thank Rebecca. Thanks for agreeing to write a book with me. For helping me push it at readers. For dealing with my bossy, nitpicky personality. (I'm that way always, but when I work... oof... I wouldn't want to deal with me AT ALL... lol) Thanks for answering a million questions about military life in the middle of the night so Iker could be an authentic hero as possible. Thanks for being the best neighbor and friend a gal could ask for. You're awesome... I mean it. One day you'll believe me when I tell you that.

I love my editor, Elaine York. I love how she makes each book I send her better, and forces me to think harder, longer, deeper about each story we work on together. She's the best. She also makes the guts of my books really pretty, so she's basically my secret weapon!

Thank you to Jenn Wood~ for digging in and copyediting BIL! Sorry I'm the world's worst at writing run-on sentences. I'd say it's part of my charm, but really, I know it is just annoying...lol.

Also thank you to Mayhem Cover Creations~ for making the outside of the book as beautiful as the inside.

Shout out to my team, Mel and Stacey. Girls rule the world, and none of these words would be in your hands without these wonderful women I get to work with day-in and day out.

Lastly, the biggest thanks go out to the readers who pre-ordered *Last Letter* and *Justified* so they could experience this co-writing journey with Rebecca and me in real time. Thank you for trusting us to give you a great story. Thank you for your support. Thank you for your excitement... thank you for reading! YOU ARE AMAZING!!!!

Acknowledgments, take two:

First up, thank you to Jason for being the soldier I met in a bar nineteen years ago. You still get me, baby.

Next and bigger thanks go to Jay, not just for the sheer amazingness of you writing this with me, but for suggesting it in the first place. For putting your name next to mine. For giving me a safe, quiet space whenever I need it. For answering every time I call, even though you hate the phone. For driving the minivan when needed and never forgetting a kid at cross-country practice while pulling off your best nanny impression. For showing up time and again and making me do the same. For being the wolf to my rabbit, and the tough love when I've had it with the universe. Secret's out, lady. You're a pineapple. Also, I'm not saying that I haven't forgiven you for the Kpop docu-drama experience of 2018, but I am saying you may have forfeited all movie choices for the next five years.

Thank you to my kids. I really appreciate the decreased time at the orthopedist, so let's keep that up, shall we? In all honesty, you are the best of me and teach me far more than I could ever hope to teach you.

Elaine, thank you for editing this for us and making sense out of our little co-written baby! Jenn, thank you for copyediting and not mocking me for my love affair with commas. LJ, I adore our cover, and every other one you've done for me! Shelby, thank you for chasing my squirrels. I promised you to keep them under control, but we both knew that would be a lie. Here's to the military guys we love.

To the readers, man, you guys ROCK for coming on this little trip with us. Thank you for preordering *The Last Letter* and *Justified*.

Also, let's be clear: Jay made me spell Luv that way. She also dresses my daughter in Kpop shirts, yeah... it's easier if you just smile and nod. ;)

About the Authors

*NEW YORK TIMES & USA TODAY BESTSELLING AUTHOR*Jay Crownover is the international and multiple *New York Times* and *USA Today* bestselling author of the Marked Men series, The Saints of Denver series, The Point series, Breaking Point series, and the Getaway series. Her books can be found translated in many different languages all around the world. She is a tattooed, crazy-haired, Colorado native, who lives at the base of the Rockies with her awesome dogs. This is where she can frequently be found enjoying a cold beer and Taco Tuesdays. Jay is a self-declared music snob and outspoken book lover who is always looking for her next adventure, between the pages and on the road.

This is the link to join my amazing fan group on Facebook: https://www.facebook.com/groups/crownoverscrowd ... I'm very active in the group, and it's often the best place to find all the latest happenings including: release dates, cover reveals, early teasers, and giveaways!

My website is:_www.jaycrownover.com and there is a link on the site to reach me through email. I would also suggest signing up for my newsletter while you're there! It's monthly, contains a free book that is in progress so you'll be the first to read it, and is full of mega giveaways and goodies. I'm also in these places:

MEET REBECCA YARROS

Rebecca Yarros is a hopeless romantic and a lover of all things coffee and chocolate. She is the author of the award-winning Flight & Glory series and The Renegades. She loves military heroes, and has been blissfully married to her Apache pilot for seventeen years.

When she's not writing, she's tying hockey skates for her four sons, sneaking in guitar time, or watching brat-pack movies with her two daughters. She lives in Colorado with her husband, their rambunctious gaggle of kids, and their menagerie of pets. Having adopted their youngest daughter from the foster system, Rebecca is a passionate advocate for children through her non-profit, One October.

Follow me on Twitter: https://twitter.com/
RebeccaYarros
Follow me on Instagram: https://www.instagram.com/
rebeccayarros/
For deleted scenes, blogs about our insane little life, and
my signing schedule, hop over to Rebeccayarros.com!